HISTORY'S KID HEROES

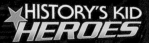

THE SNOWSHOEING ADVENTURE OF MILTON DAUB, BLIZZARD TREKKER

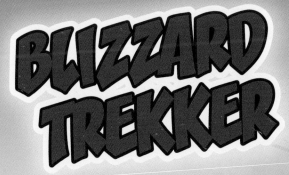

BY MARGARET K. WETTERER AND CHARLES M. WETTERER
ADAPTATION BY EMMA CARLSON BERNE
ILLLUSTRATED BY ZACHARY TROVER

Graphic Universe™ Minneapolis • New York

INTRODUCTION

FOR THREE DAYS IN MARCH 1888, A BLIZZARD RAGED THROUGHOUT THE NORTHEASTERN UNITED STATES. SNOW AND ICE BURIED THE LAND FROM MAINE TO MARYLAND. ROADS WERE CLOSED, AND HUNDREDS OF PASSENGER TRAINS WERE STUCK FOR DAYS BEHIND HUGE SNOWDRIFTS. WINDS, SOME OVER 80 MILES PER HOUR, CRACKED WINDOWS, TORE AWAY FENCES, ROOFS, AND SIGNS, AND TOPPLED TREES AND UTILITY POLES. THOUSANDS OF BIRDS FELL FROZEN FROM BUSHES AND BUILDINGS WHERE THEY HAD HUDDLED FOR SHELTER. MILES OF TELEPHONE AND TELEGRAPH WIRES SNAPPED UNDER THE PRESSURE OF WIND, ICE, AND SNOW.

CITIES, TOWNS, FARMS, AND FAMILIES WERE CUT OFF FROM ONE ANOTHER. FOR A TIME, THE GOVERNMENT IN WASHINGTON, D.C., LOST ALL CONTACT WITH THE REST OF THE COUNTRY. AT SEA, VIOLENT WINDS

AND WAVES DAMAGED COUNTLESS BOATS AND SANK MORE THAN TWO HUNDRED OF THEM.

MILTON DAUB WAS 12 YEARS OLD WHEN THE STORM STRUCK. HE AND HIS FAMILY LIVED IN THE BRONX, A TOWN THAT HAD BECOME PART OF NEW YORK CITY A FEW YEARS BEFORE. AT THE TIME, THE BRONX HAD A SMALL BUSINESS AND RESIDENTIAL CENTER WITH MILES OF FIELDS AND FARMS TO THE NORTH. THE DAUBS' TWO-STORY WOOD-FRAME HOUSE FACED 145TH STREET, A WIDE DIRT ROAD. MILTON WAS THE OLDEST OF FIVE CHILDREN. HE HAD TWO SISTERS, ELLA AND HANNAH, AND TWO BROTHERS, MAURICE AND JEROME.

THIS IS THE STORY OF MILTON DAUB'S ADVENTURE IN THAT TERRIBLE STORM, KNOWN EVER AFTER AS THE GREAT BLIZZARD OF '88.

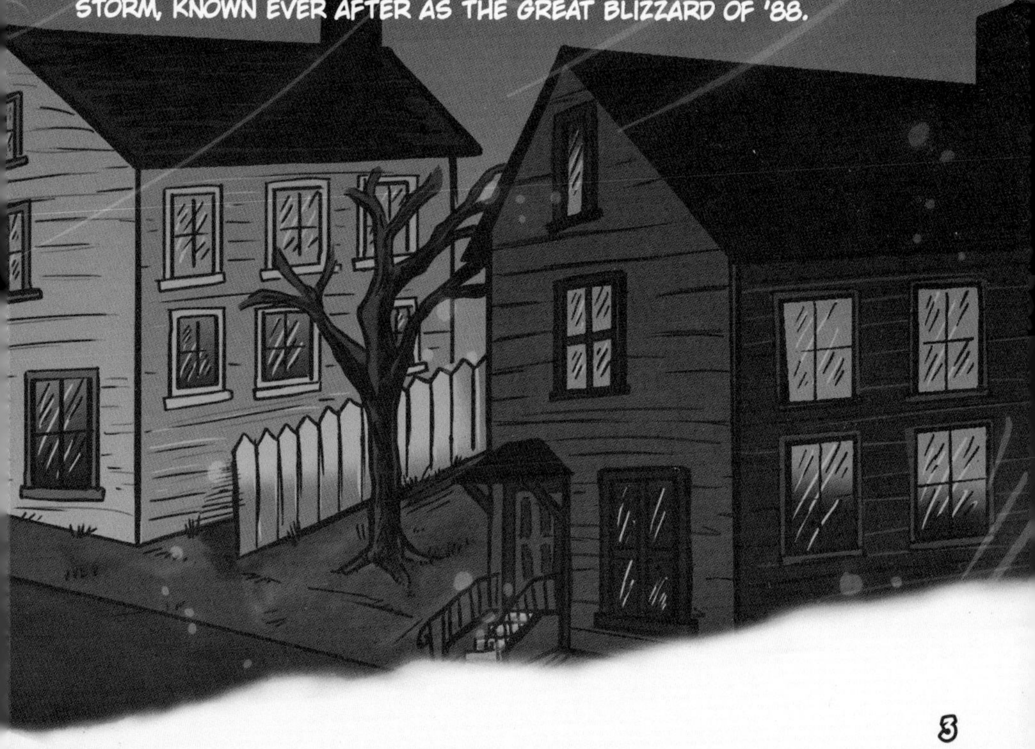

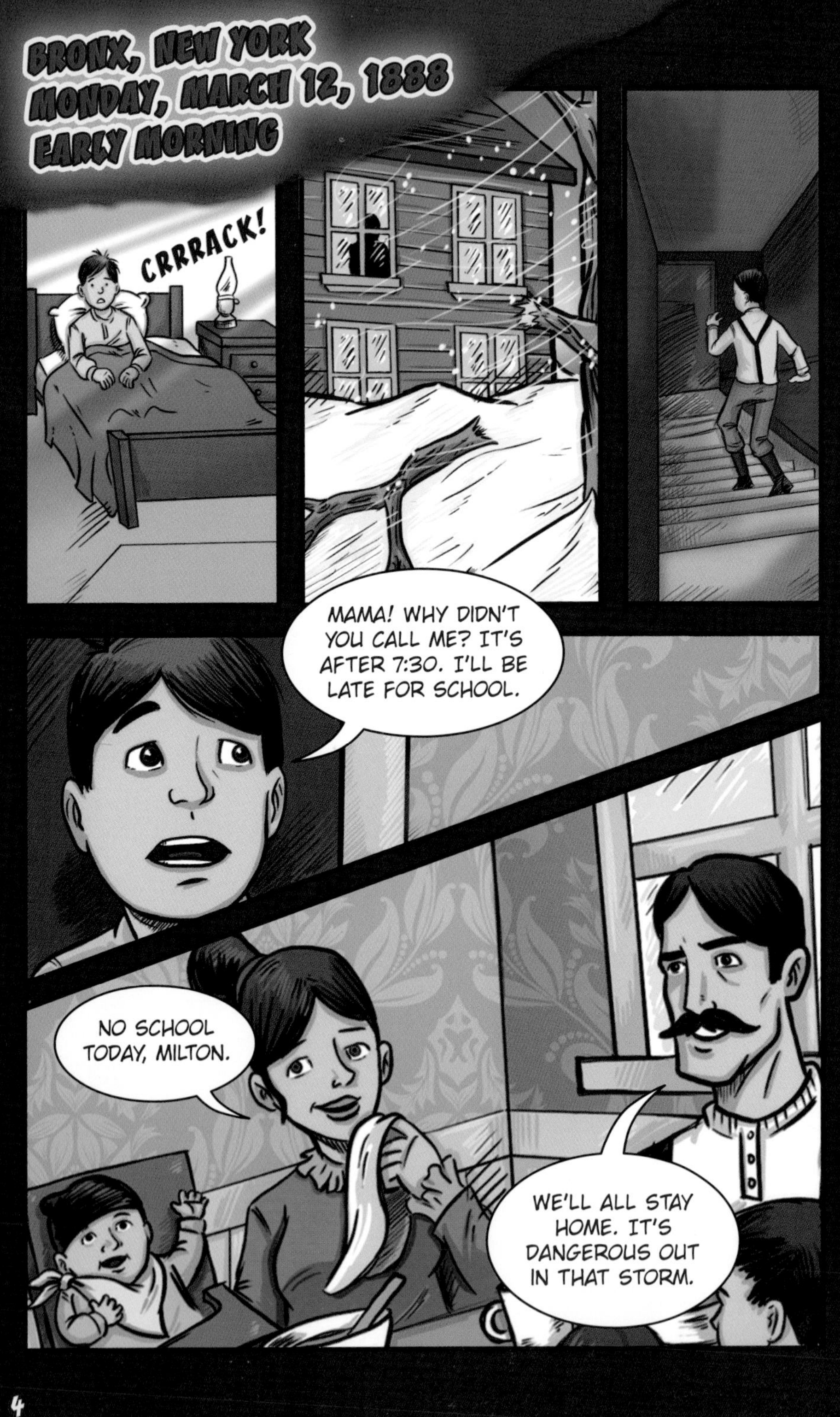
BRONX, NEW YORK
MONDAY, MARCH 12, 1888
EARLY MORNING
CRRRACK!
MAMA! WHY DIDN'T YOU CALL ME? IT'S AFTER 7:30. I'LL BE LATE FOR SCHOOL.
NO SCHOOL TODAY, MILTON.
WE'LL ALL STAY HOME. IT'S DANGEROUS OUT IN THAT STORM.

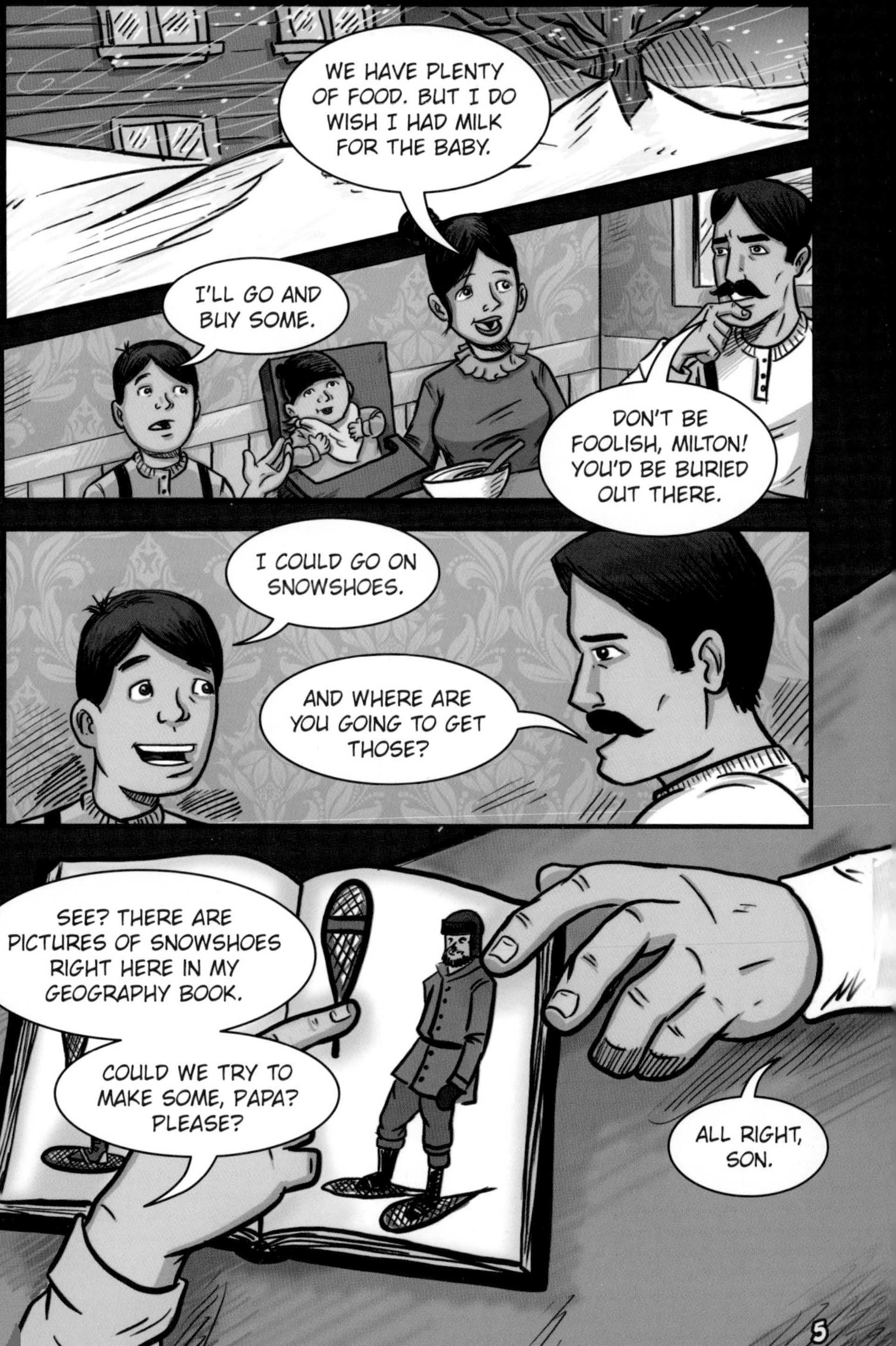
WE HAVE PLENTY OF FOOD. BUT I DO WISH I HAD MILK FOR THE BABY.
I'LL GO AND BUY SOME.
DON'T BE FOOLISH, MILTON! YOU'D BE BURIED OUT THERE.
I COULD GO ON SNOWSHOES.
AND WHERE ARE YOU GOING TO GET THOSE?
SEE? THERE ARE PICTURES OF SNOWSHOES RIGHT HERE IN MY GEOGRAPHY BOOK.
COULD WE TRY TO MAKE SOME, PAPA? PLEASE?
ALL RIGHT, SON.

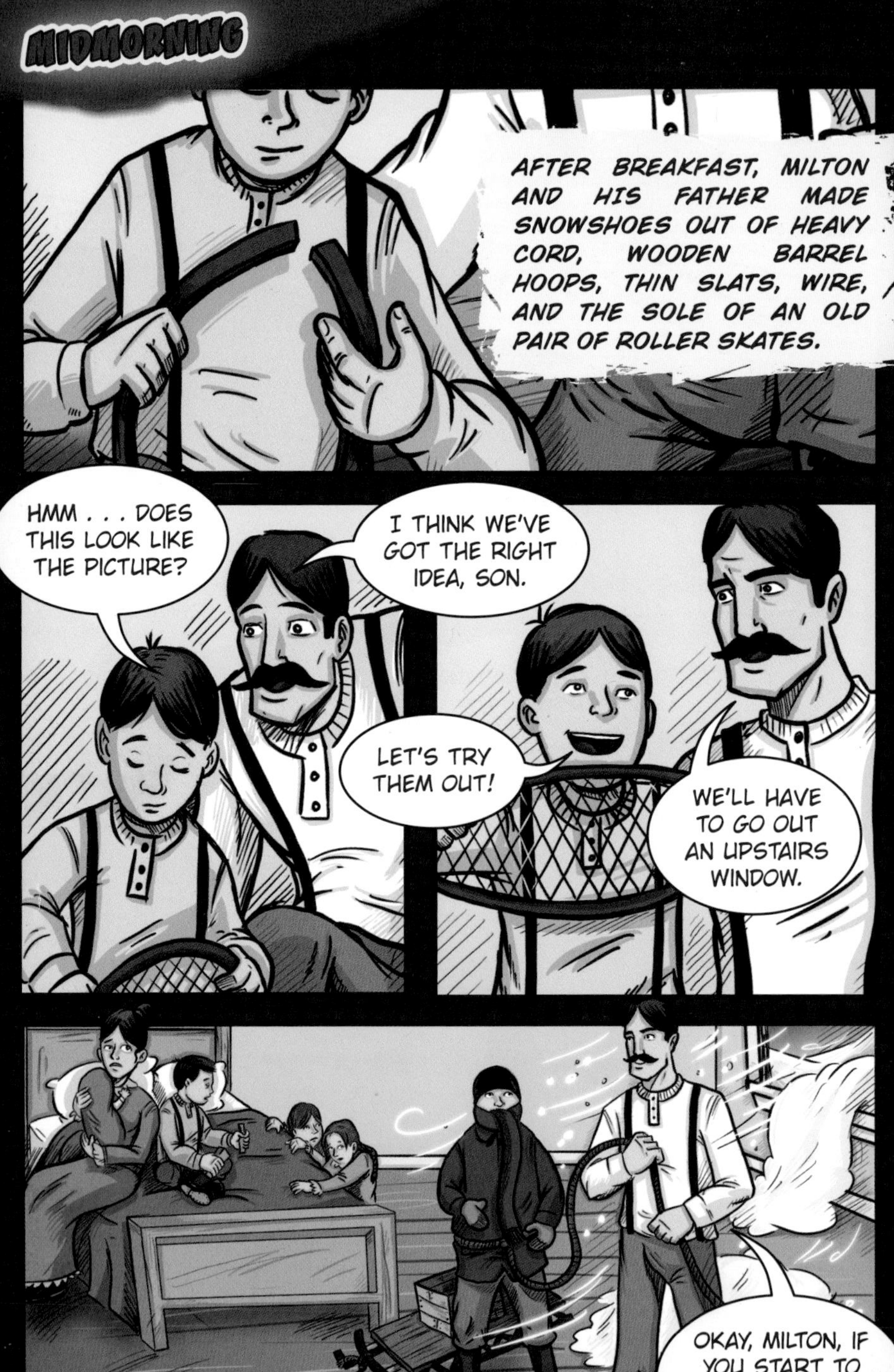
MIDMORNING
AFTER BREAKFAST, MILTON AND HIS FATHER MADE SNOWSHOES OUT OF HEAVY CORD, WOODEN BARREL HOOPS, THIN SLATS, WIRE, AND THE SOLE OF AN OLD PAIR OF ROLLER SKATES.
HMM . . . DOES THIS LOOK LIKE THE PICTURE?
I THINK WE'VE GOT THE RIGHT IDEA, SON.
LET'S TRY THEM OUT!
WE'LL HAVE TO GO OUT AN UPSTAIRS WINDOW.
OKAY, MILTON, IF YOU START TO SINK, I'LL PULL YOU BACK.

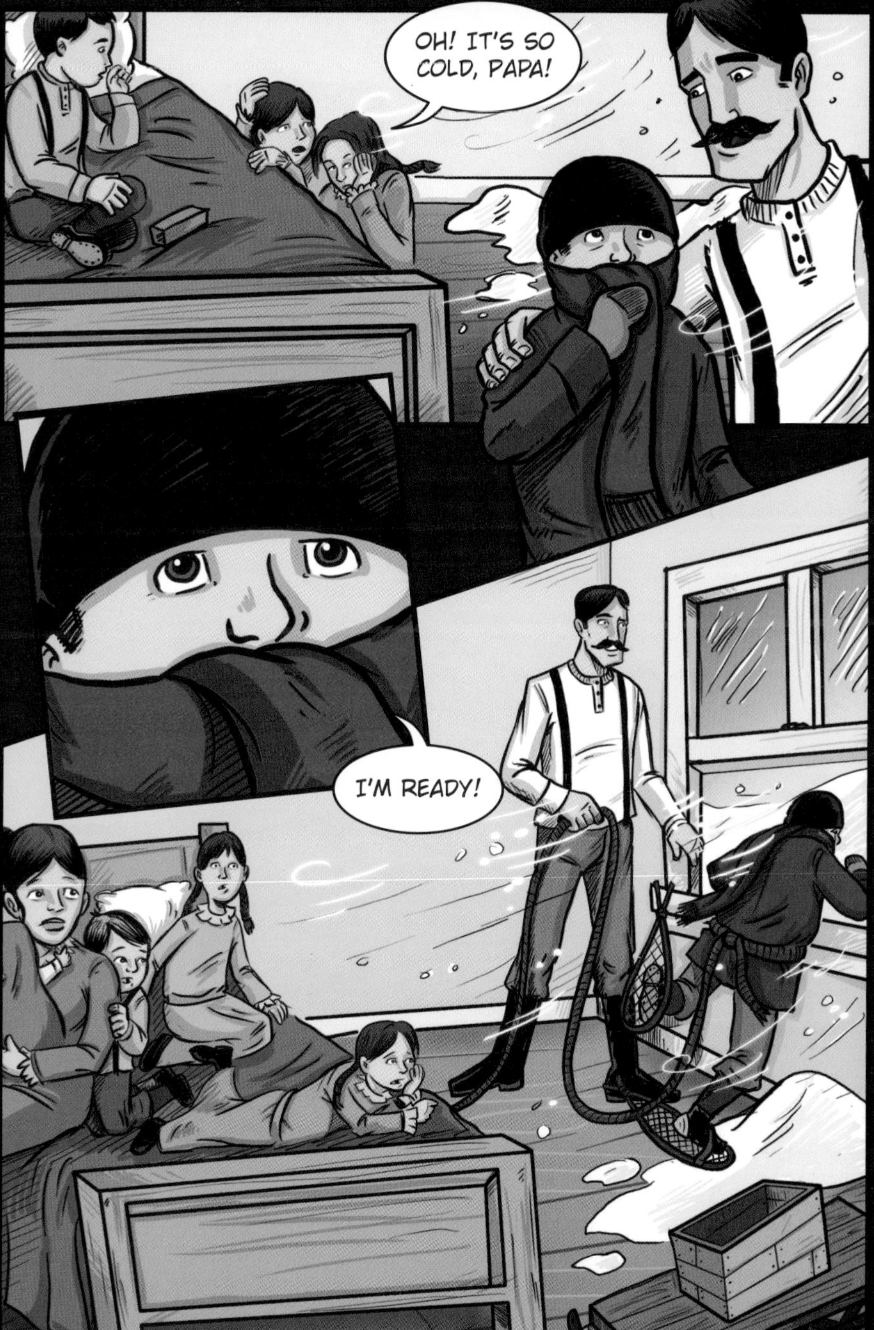
OH! IT'S SO COLD, PAPA!
I'M READY!

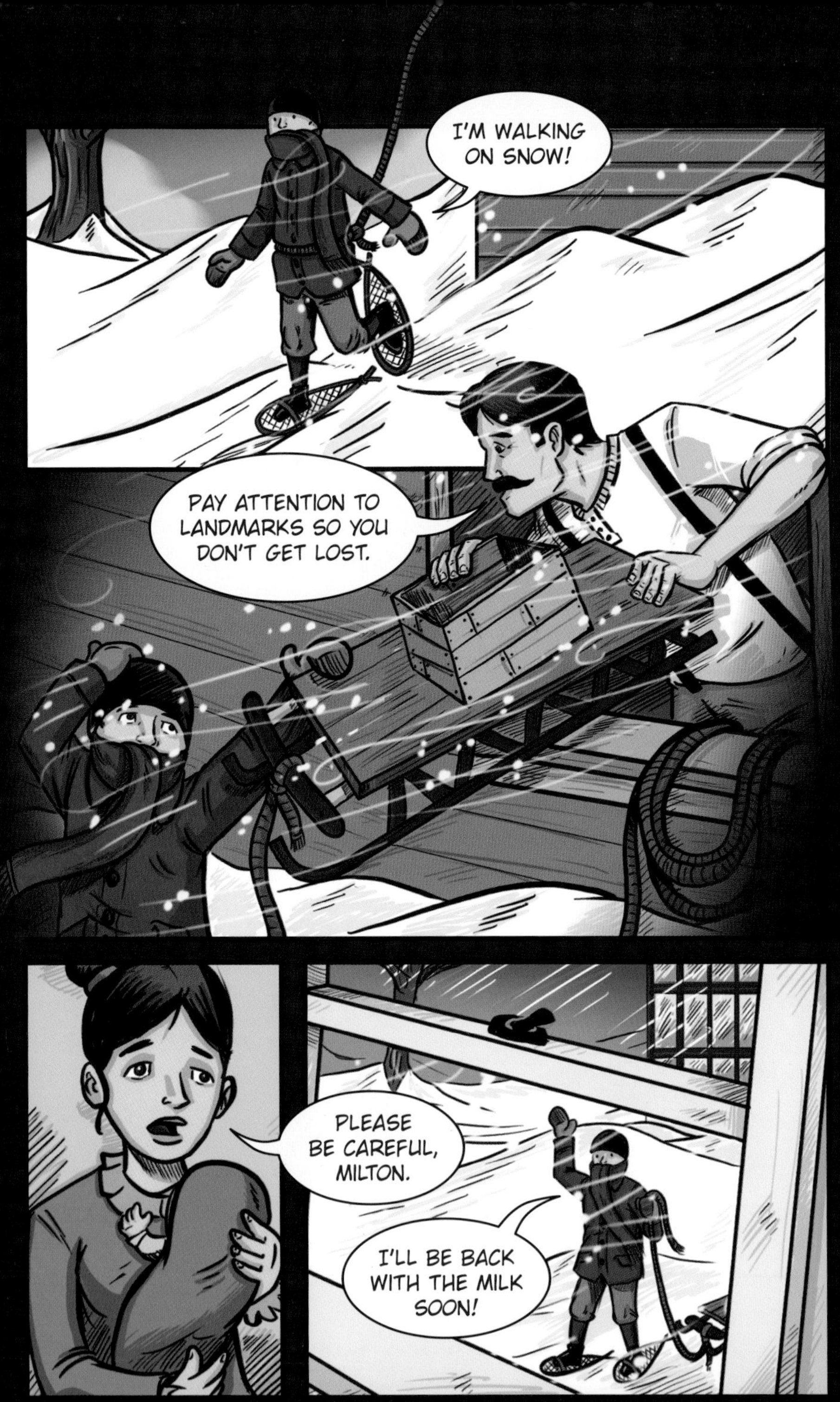
I'M WALKING ON SNOW!
PAY ATTENTION TO LANDMARKS SO YOU DON'T GET LOST.
PLEASE BE CAREFUL, MILTON.
I'LL BE BACK WITH THE MILK SOON!

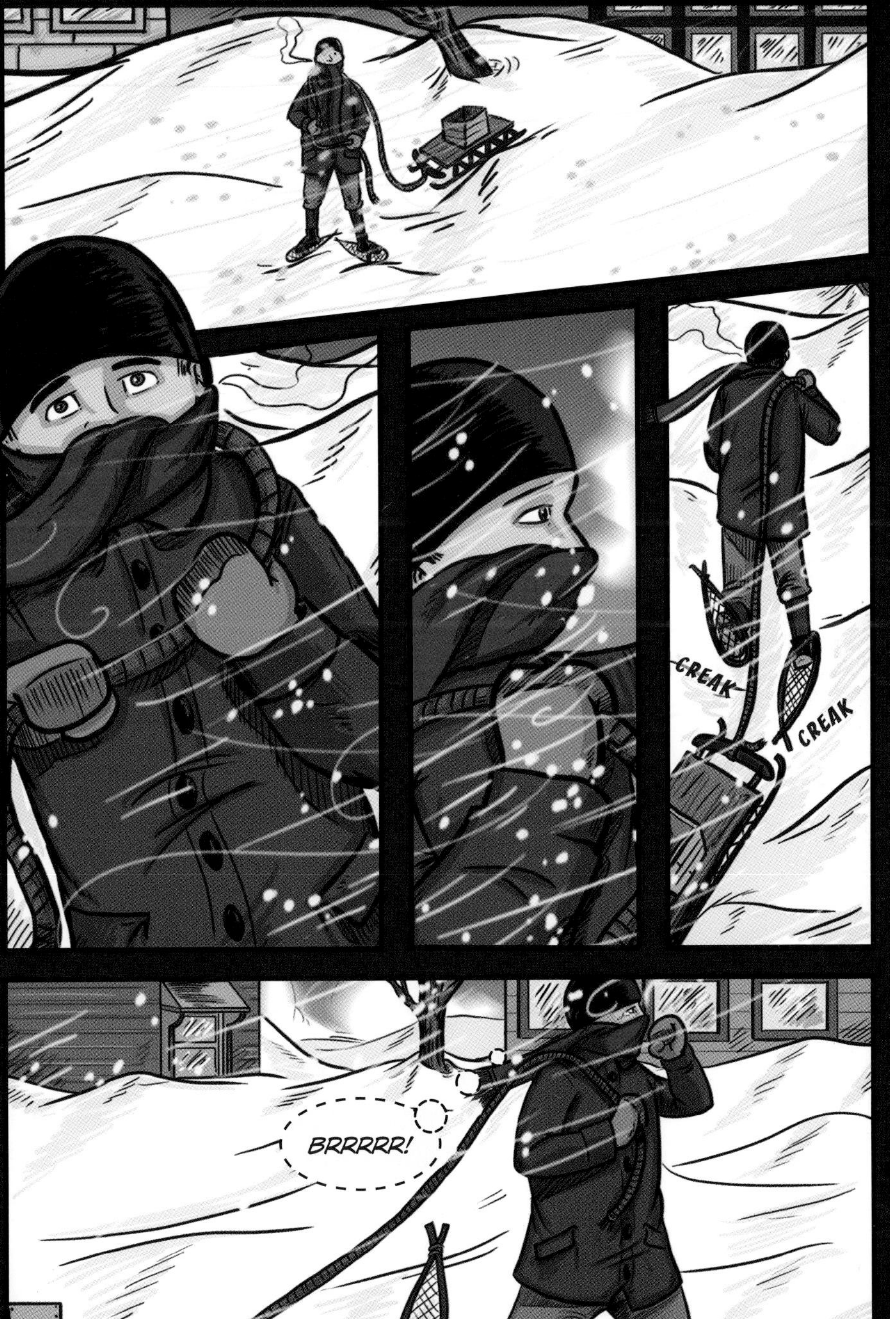
CREAK
CREAK
BRRRRR!

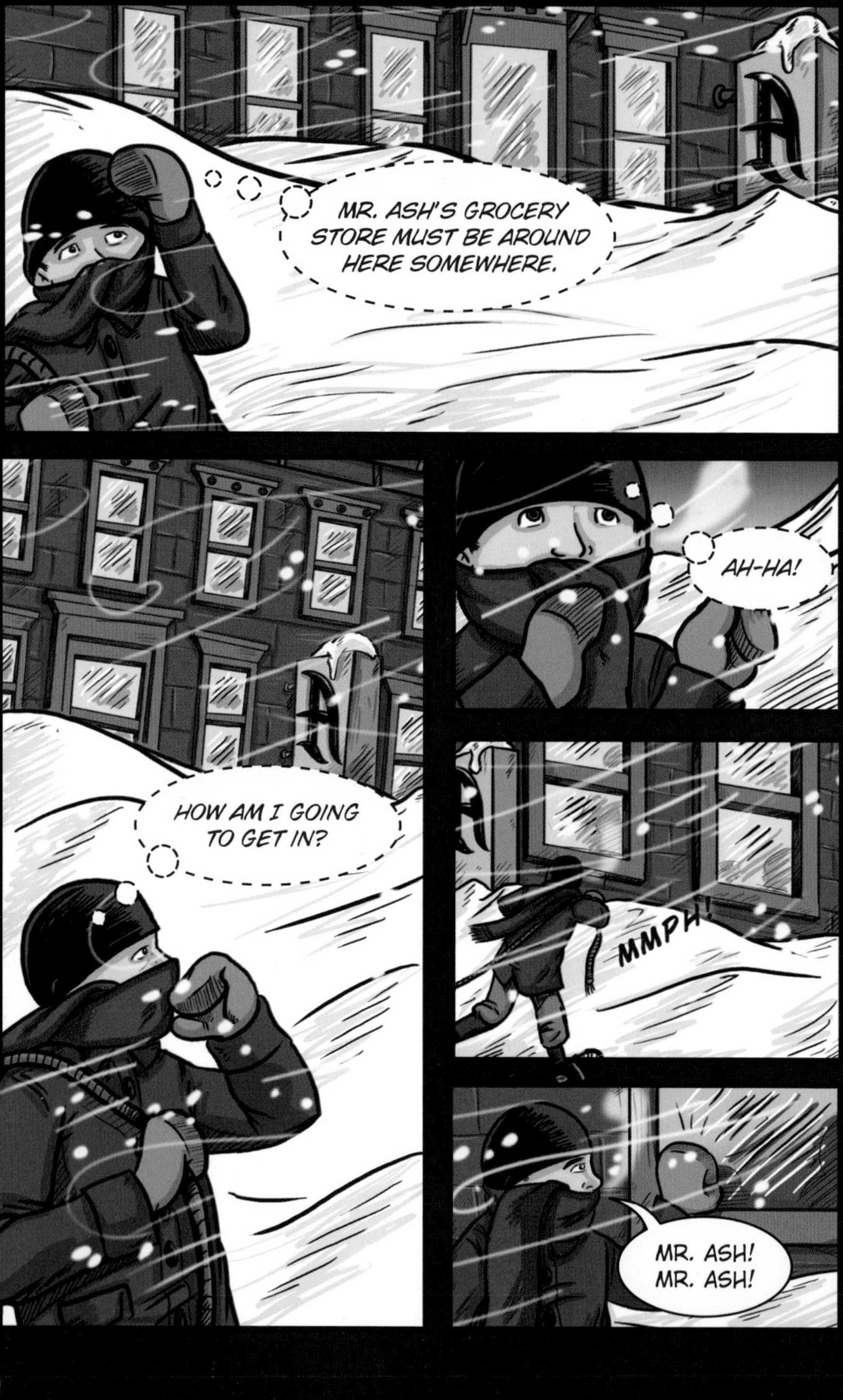
MR. ASH'S GROCERY STORE MUST BE AROUND HERE SOMEWHERE.
HOW AM I GOING TO GET IN?
AH-HA!
MMPH!
MR. ASH! MR. ASH!

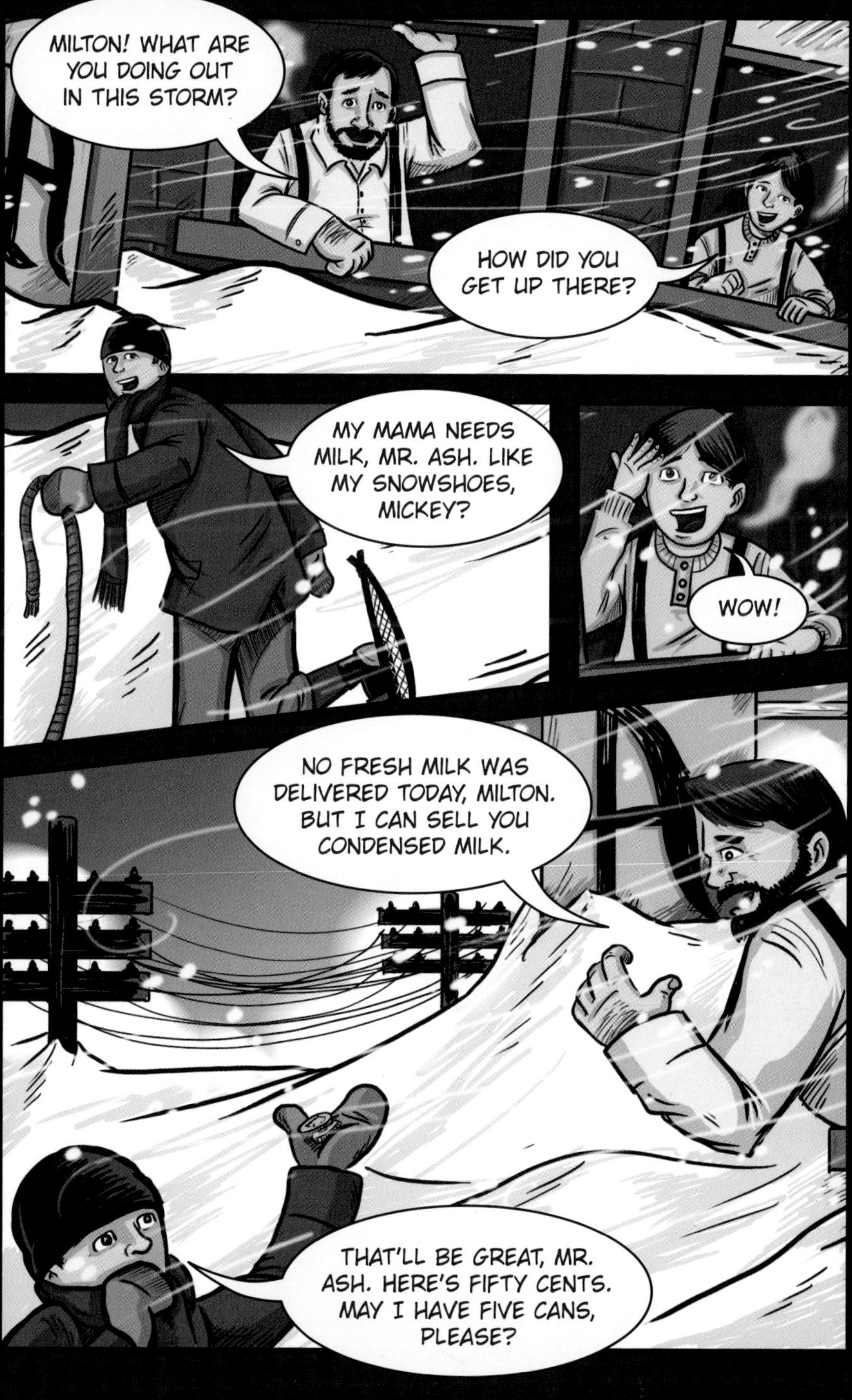
MILTON! WHAT ARE YOU DOING OUT IN THIS STORM?
HOW DID YOU GET UP THERE?
MY MAMA NEEDS MILK, MR. ASH. LIKE MY SNOWSHOES, MICKEY?
WOW!
NO FRESH MILK WAS DELIVERED TODAY, MILTON. BUT I CAN SELL YOU CONDENSED MILK.
THAT'LL BE GREAT, MR. ASH. HERE'S FIFTY CENTS. MAY I HAVE FIVE CANS, PLEASE?

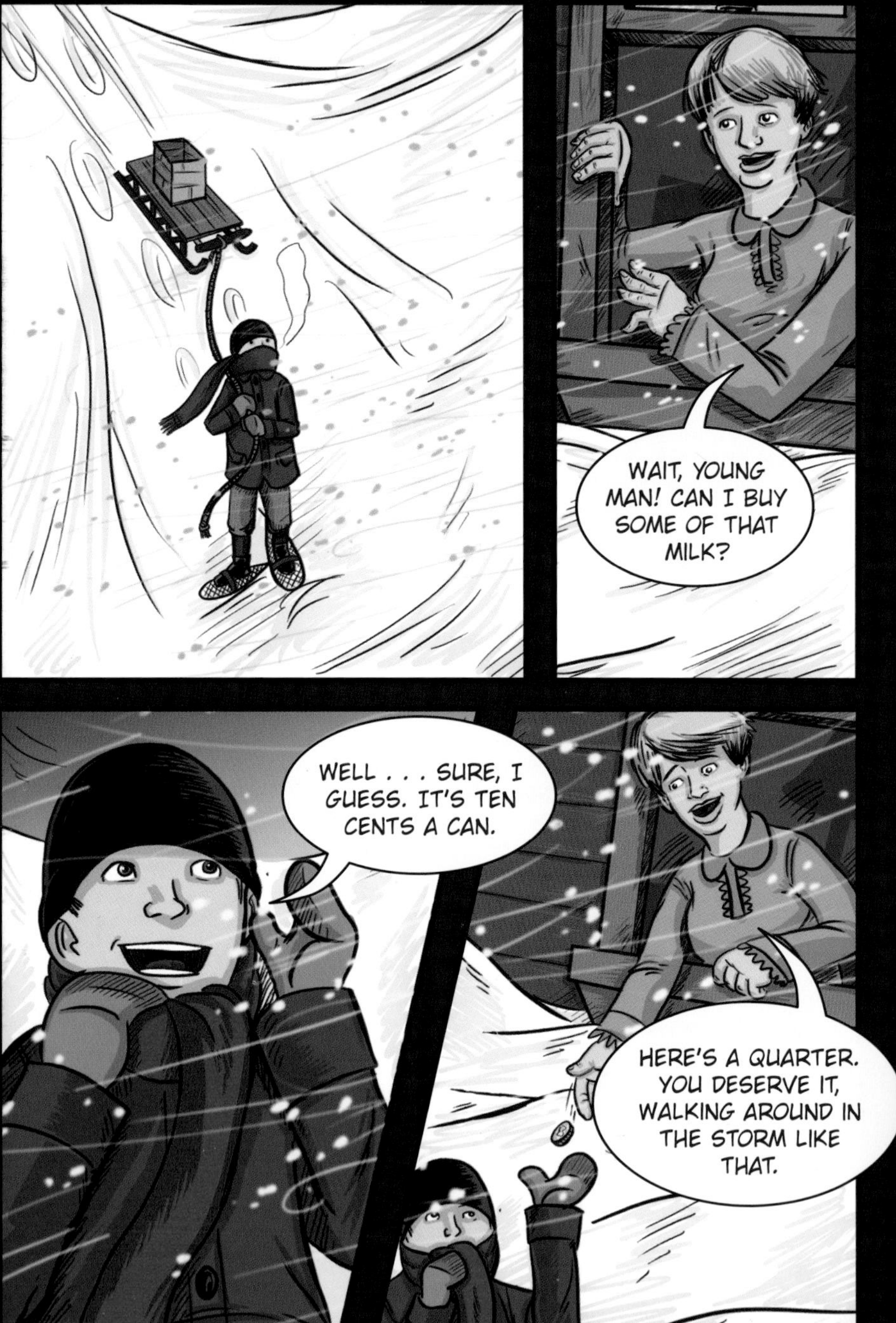
WAIT, YOUNG MAN! CAN I BUY SOME OF THAT MILK?
WELL . . . SURE, I GUESS. IT'S TEN CENTS A CAN.
HERE'S A QUARTER. YOU DESERVE IT, WALKING AROUND IN THE STORM LIKE THAT.

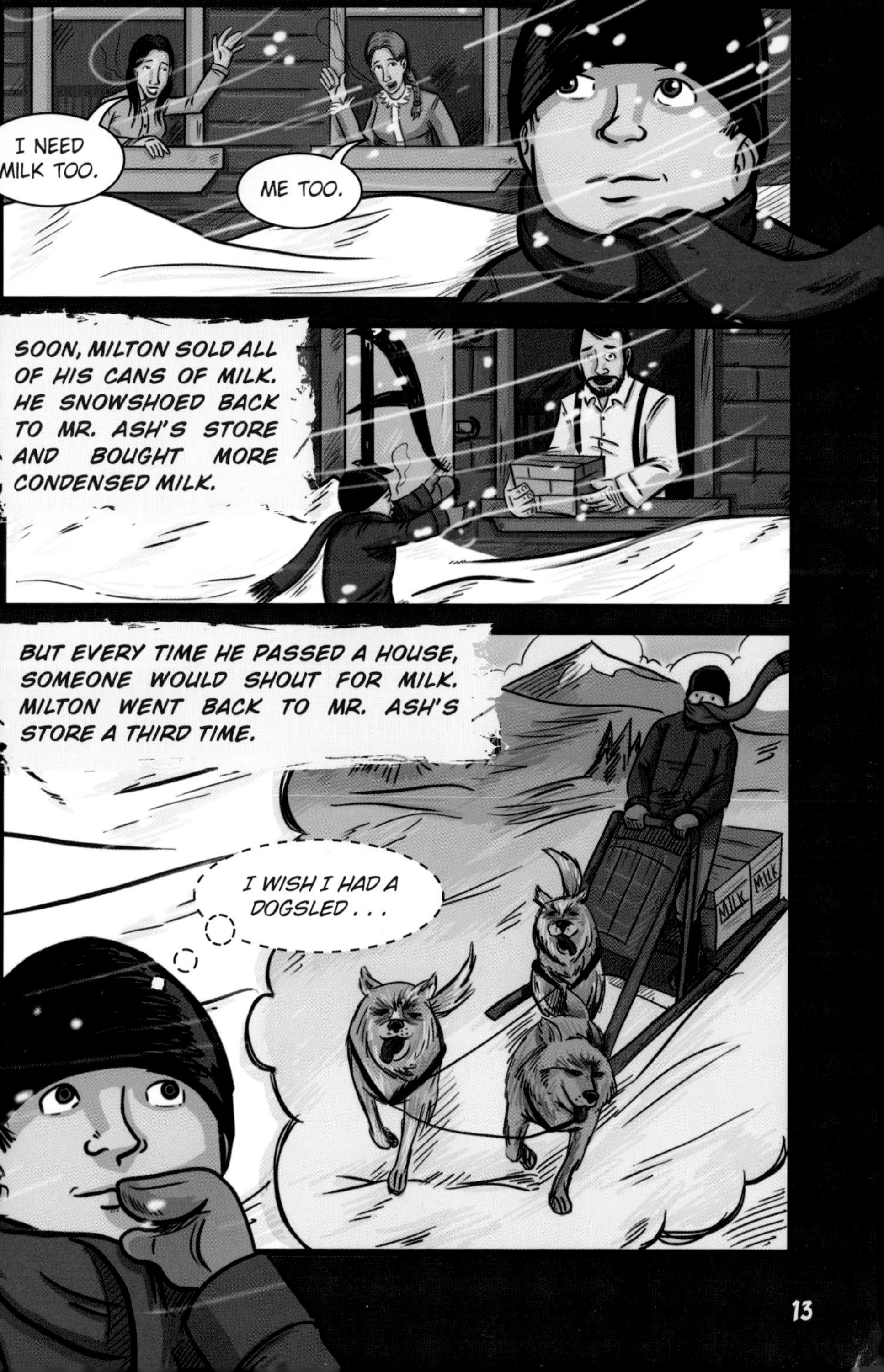
I NEED MILK TOO.
ME TOO.
SOON, MILTON SOLD ALL OF HIS CANS OF MILK. HE SNOWSHOED BACK TO MR. ASH'S STORE AND BOUGHT MORE CONDENSED MILK.
BUT EVERY TIME HE PASSED A HOUSE, SOMEONE WOULD SHOUT FOR MILK. MILTON WENT BACK TO MR. ASH'S STORE A THIRD TIME.
I WISH I HAD A DOGSLED . . .
MILK
MILK

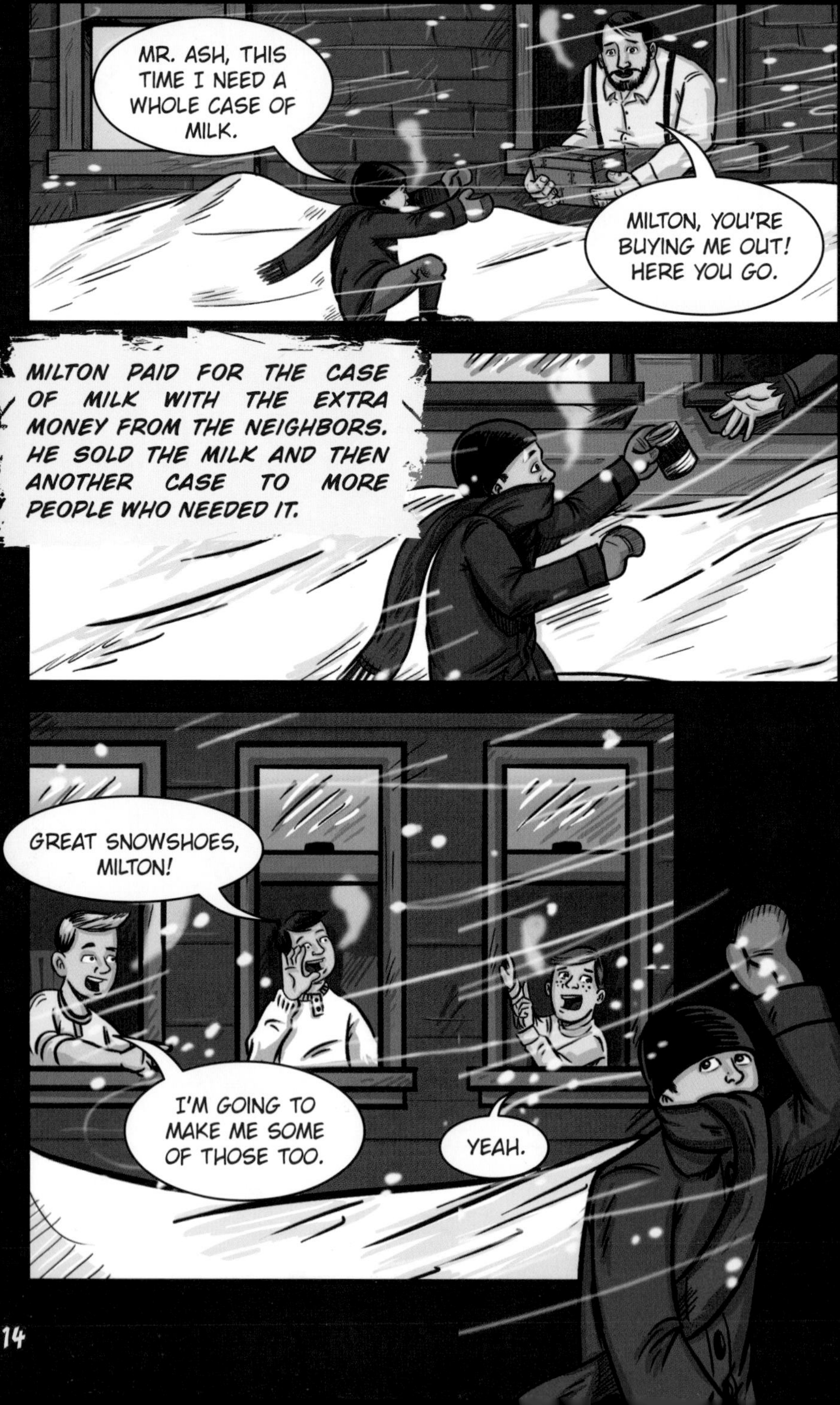
MR. ASH, THIS TIME I NEED A WHOLE CASE OF MILK.
MILTON, YOU'RE BUYING ME OUT! HERE YOU GO.
MILTON PAID FOR THE CASE OF MILK WITH THE EXTRA MONEY FROM THE NEIGHBORS. HE SOLD THE MILK AND THEN ANOTHER CASE TO MORE PEOPLE WHO NEEDED IT.
GREAT SNOWSHOES, MILTON!
I'M GOING TO MAKE ME SOME OF THOSE TOO.
YEAH.

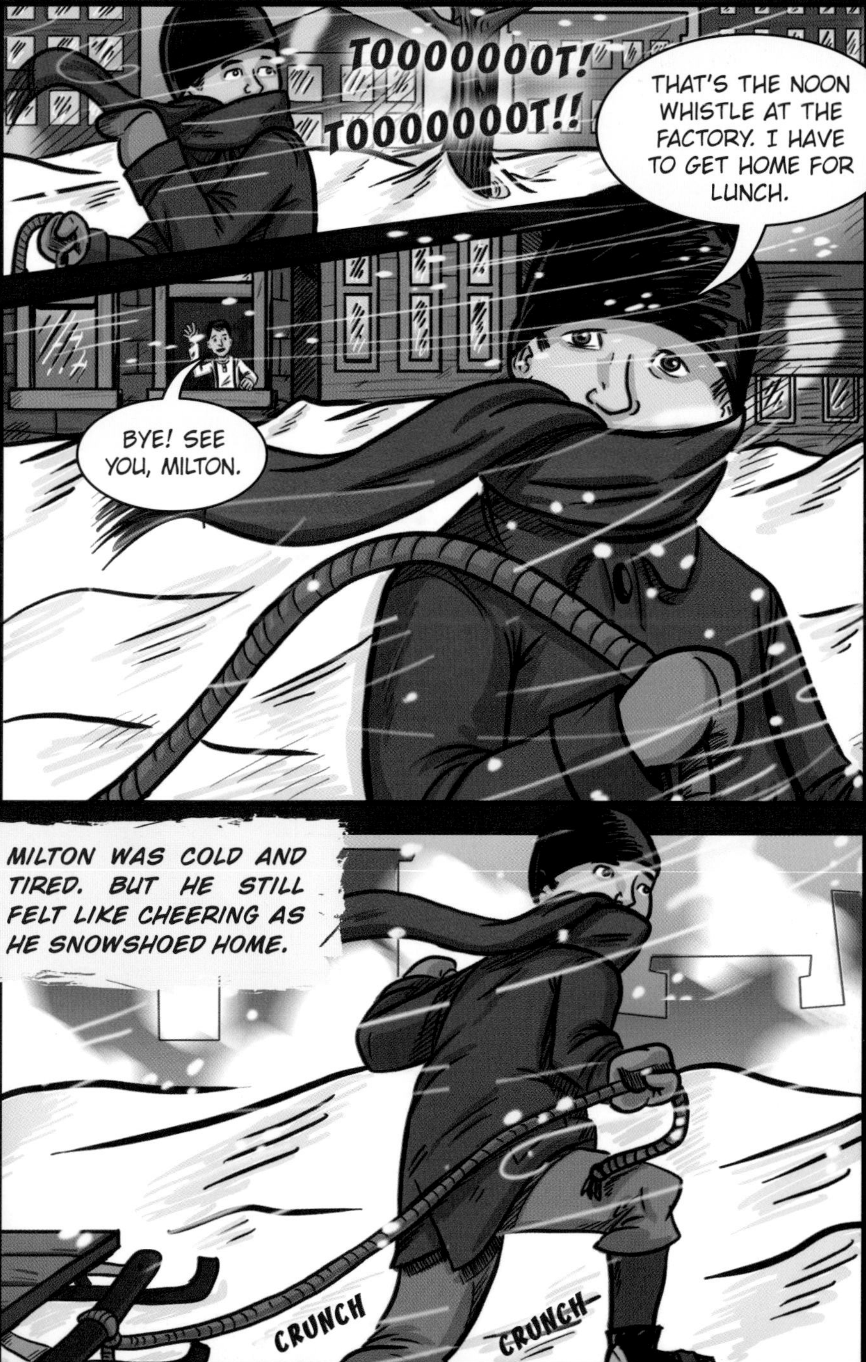
TOOOOOOOT!
TOOOOOOOT!!
THAT'S THE NOON WHISTLE AT THE FACTORY. I HAVE TO GET HOME FOR LUNCH.
BYE! SEE YOU, MILTON.
MILTON WAS COLD AND TIRED. BUT HE STILL FELT LIKE CHEERING AS HE SNOWSHOED HOME.
CRUNCH
CRUNCH

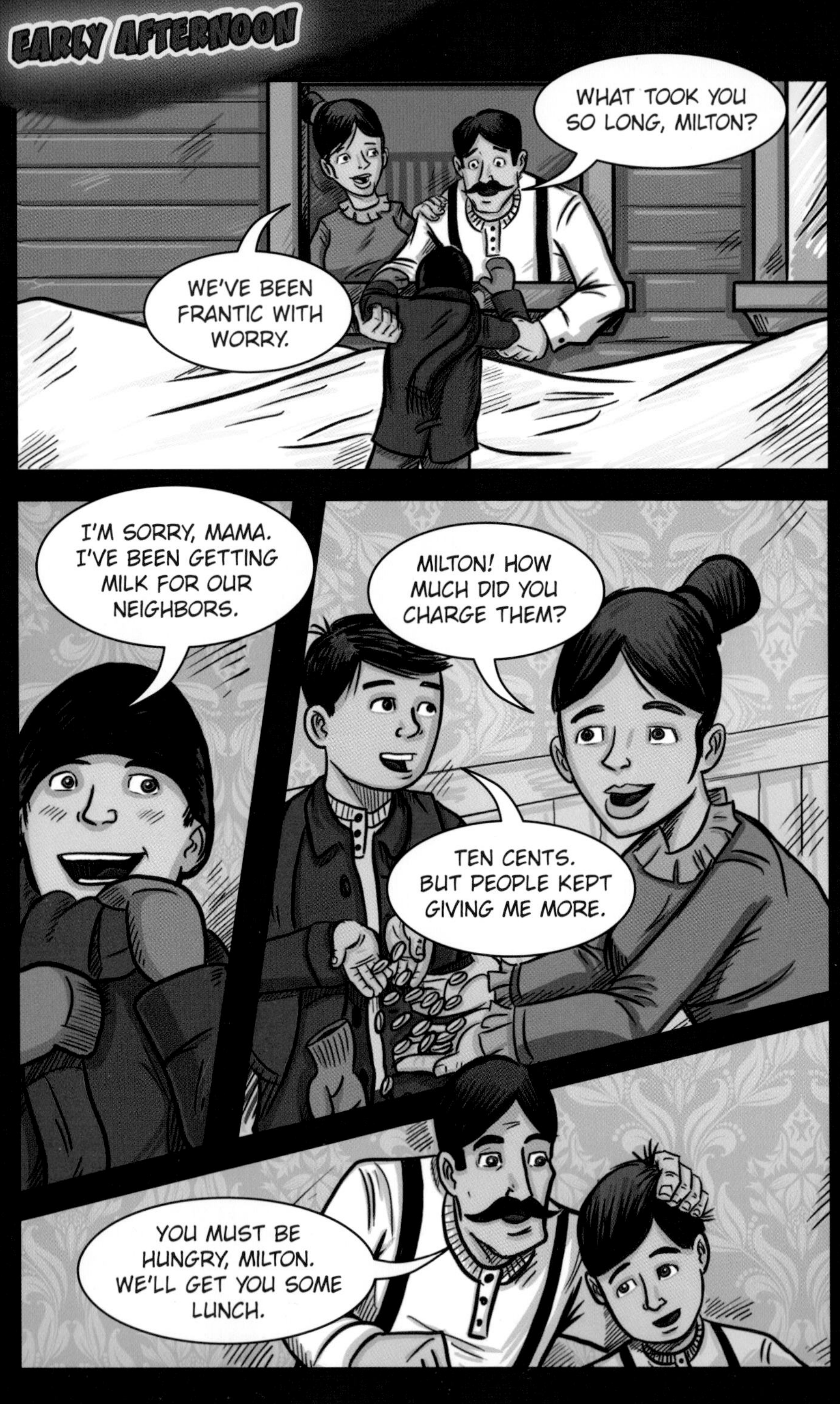
EARLY AFTERNOON
WHAT TOOK YOU SO LONG, MILTON?
WE'VE BEEN FRANTIC WITH WORRY.
I'M SORRY, MAMA. I'VE BEEN GETTING MILK FOR OUR NEIGHBORS.
MILTON! HOW MUCH DID YOU CHARGE THEM?
TEN CENTS. BUT PEOPLE KEPT GIVING ME MORE.
YOU MUST BE HUNGRY, MILTON. WE'LL GET YOU SOME LUNCH.

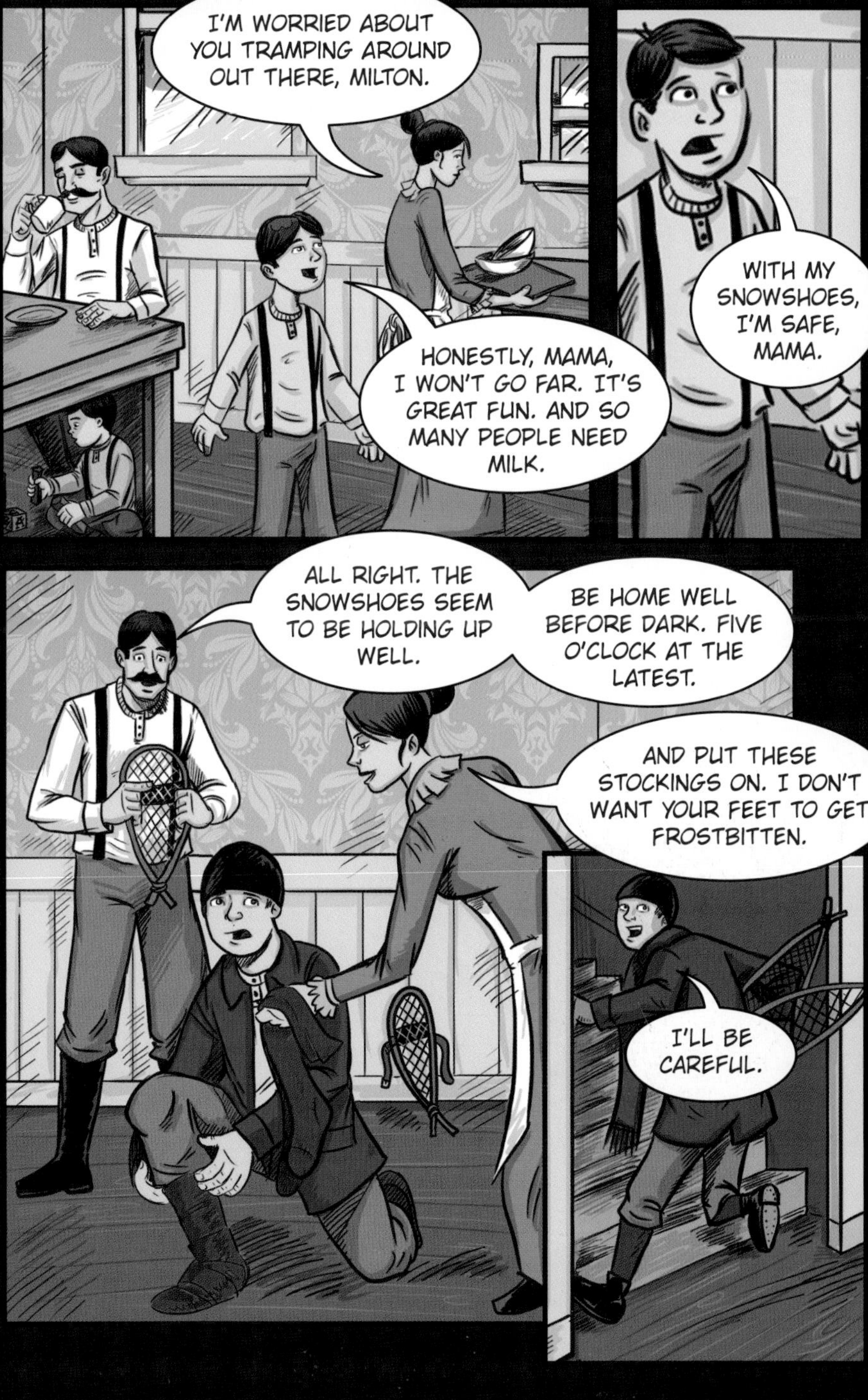
I'M WORRIED ABOUT YOU TRAMPING AROUND OUT THERE, MILTON.
HONESTLY, MAMA, I WON'T GO FAR. IT'S GREAT FUN. AND SO MANY PEOPLE NEED MILK.
WITH MY SNOWSHOES, I'M SAFE, MAMA.
ALL RIGHT. THE SNOWSHOES SEEM TO BE HOLDING UP WELL.
BE HOME WELL BEFORE DARK. FIVE O'CLOCK AT THE LATEST.
AND PUT THESE STOCKINGS ON. I DON'T WANT YOUR FEET TO GET FROSTBITTEN.
I'LL BE CAREFUL.

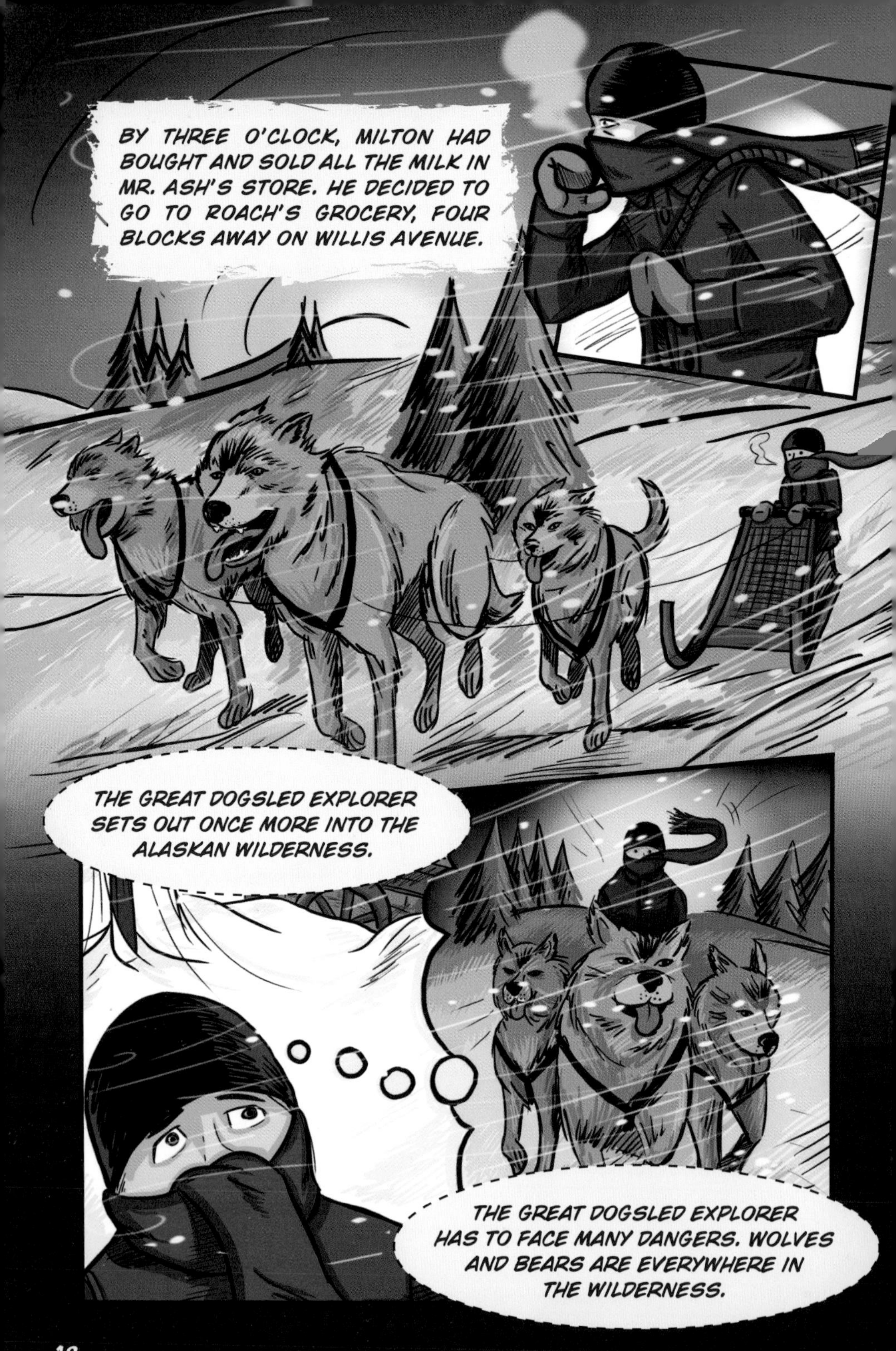
BY THREE O'CLOCK, MILTON HAD BOUGHT AND SOLD ALL THE MILK IN MR. ASH'S STORE. HE DECIDED TO GO TO ROACH'S GROCERY, FOUR BLOCKS AWAY ON WILLIS AVENUE.
THE GREAT DOGSLED EXPLORER SETS OUT ONCE MORE INTO THE ALASKAN WILDERNESS.
THE GREAT DOGSLED EXPLORER HAS TO FACE MANY DANGERS. WOLVES AND BEARS ARE EVERYWHERE IN THE WILDERNESS.

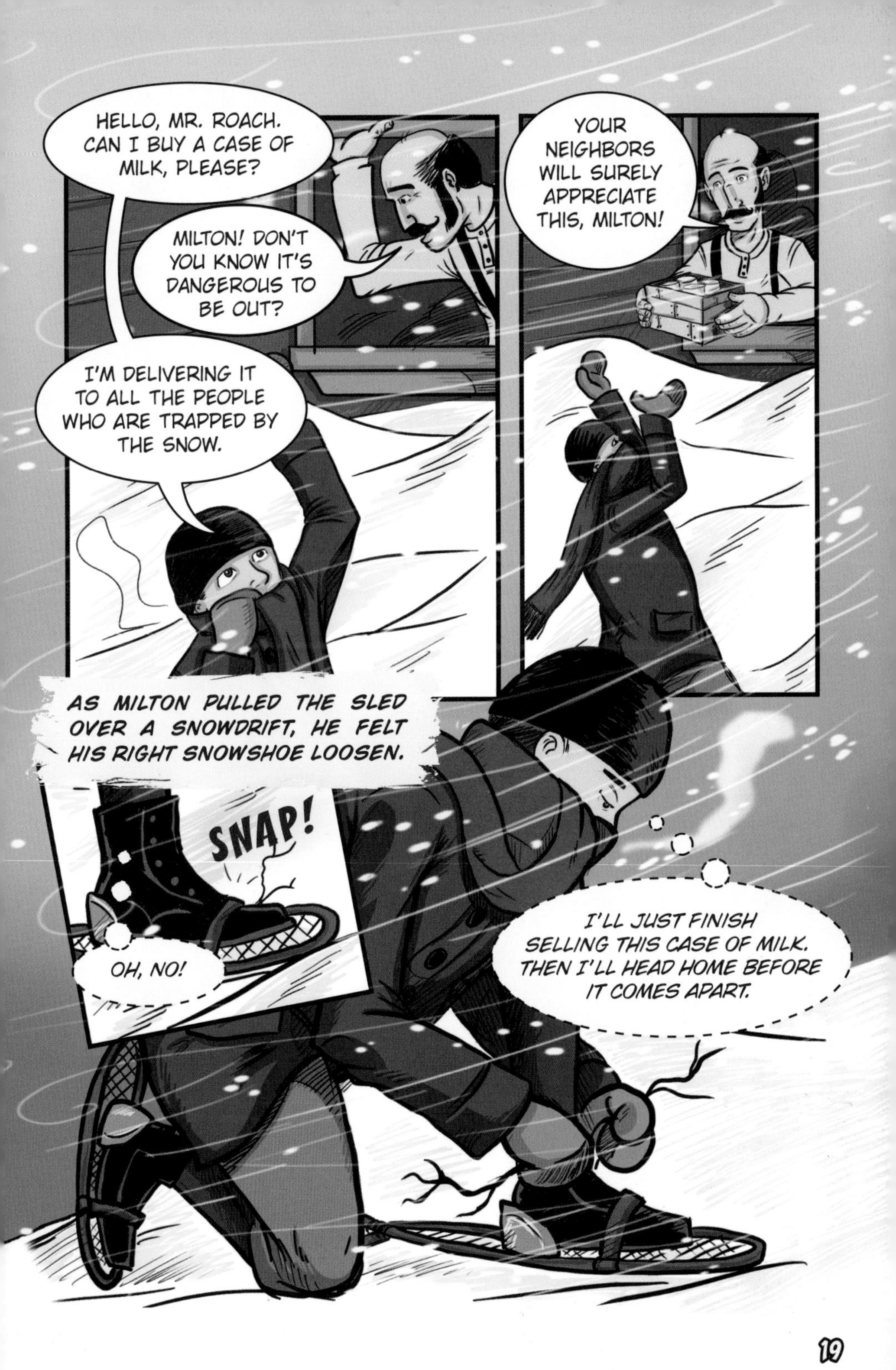
HELLO, MR. ROACH. CAN I BUY A CASE OF MILK, PLEASE?
MILTON! DON'T YOU KNOW IT'S DANGEROUS TO BE OUT?
I'M DELIVERING IT TO ALL THE PEOPLE WHO ARE TRAPPED BY THE SNOW.
YOUR NEIGHBORS WILL SURELY APPRECIATE THIS, MILTON!
AS MILTON PULLED THE SLED OVER A SNOWDRIFT, HE FELT HIS RIGHT SNOWSHOE LOOSEN.
SNAP!
OH, NO!
I'LL JUST FINISH SELLING THIS CASE OF MILK. THEN I'LL HEAD HOME BEFORE IT COMES APART.

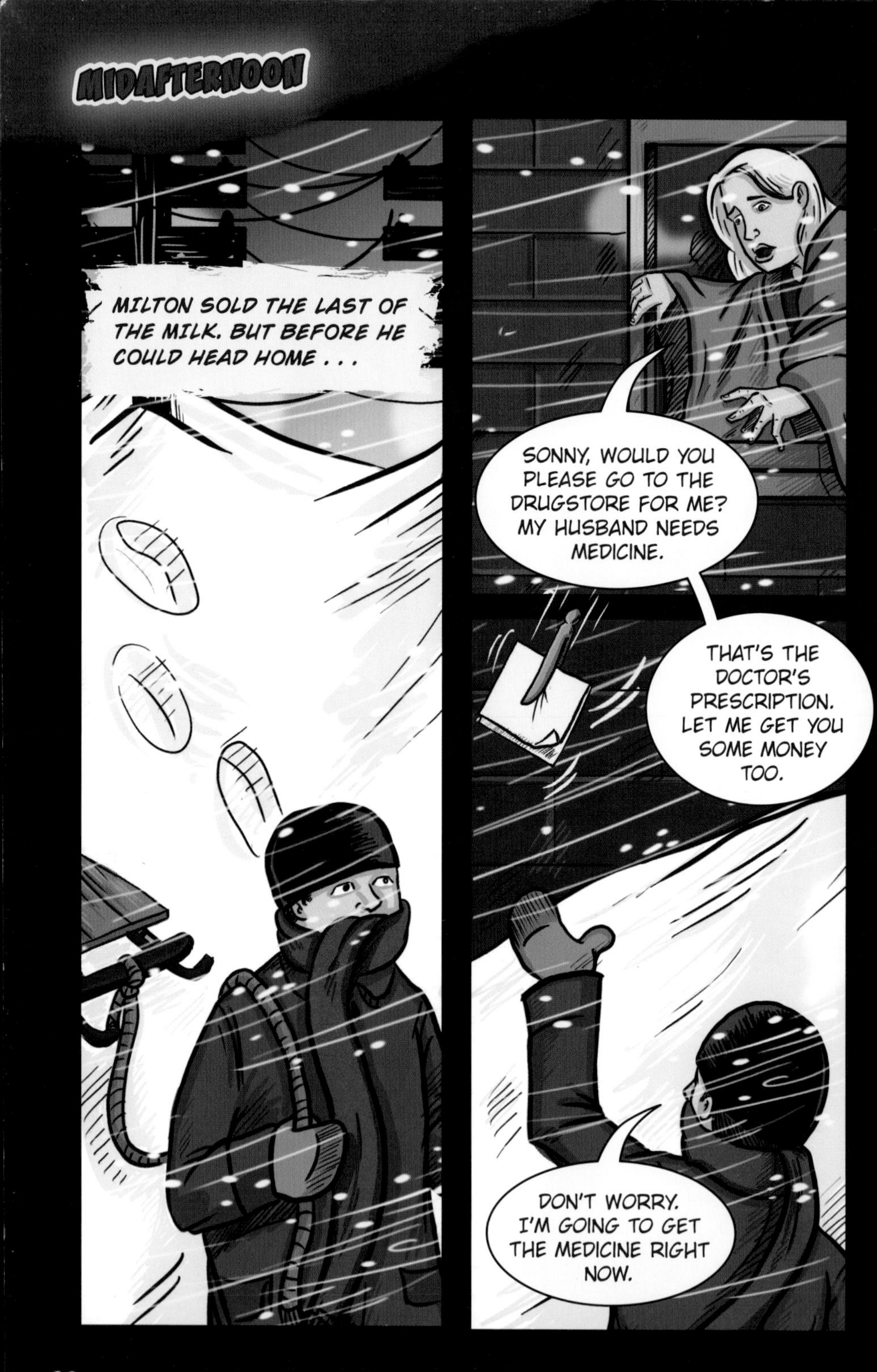
MIDAFTERNOON
MILTON SOLD THE LAST OF THE MILK. BUT BEFORE HE COULD HEAD HOME . . .
SONNY, WOULD YOU PLEASE GO TO THE DRUGSTORE FOR ME? MY HUSBAND NEEDS MEDICINE.
THAT'S THE DOCTOR'S PRESCRIPTION. LET ME GET YOU SOME MONEY TOO.
DON'T WORRY. I'M GOING TO GET THE MEDICINE RIGHT NOW.

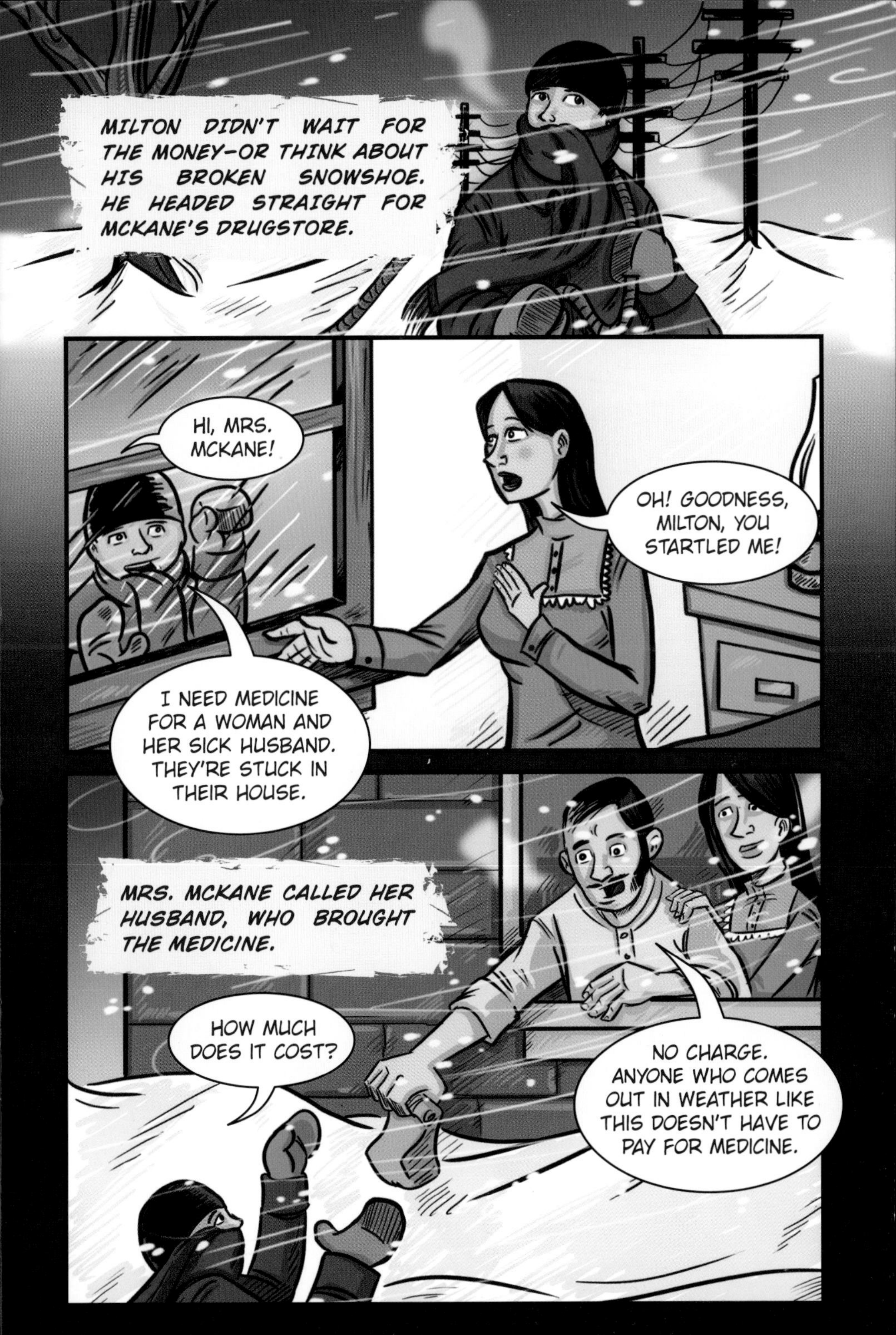
MILTON DIDN'T WAIT FOR THE MONEY—OR THINK ABOUT HIS BROKEN SNOWSHOE. HE HEADED STRAIGHT FOR MCKANE'S DRUGSTORE.
HI, MRS. MCKANE!
OH! GOODNESS, MILTON, YOU STARTLED ME!
I NEED MEDICINE FOR A WOMAN AND HER SICK HUSBAND. THEY'RE STUCK IN THEIR HOUSE.
MRS. MCKANE CALLED HER HUSBAND, WHO BROUGHT THE MEDICINE.
HOW MUCH DOES IT COST?
NO CHARGE. ANYONE WHO COMES OUT IN WEATHER LIKE THIS DOESN'T HAVE TO PAY FOR MEDICINE.

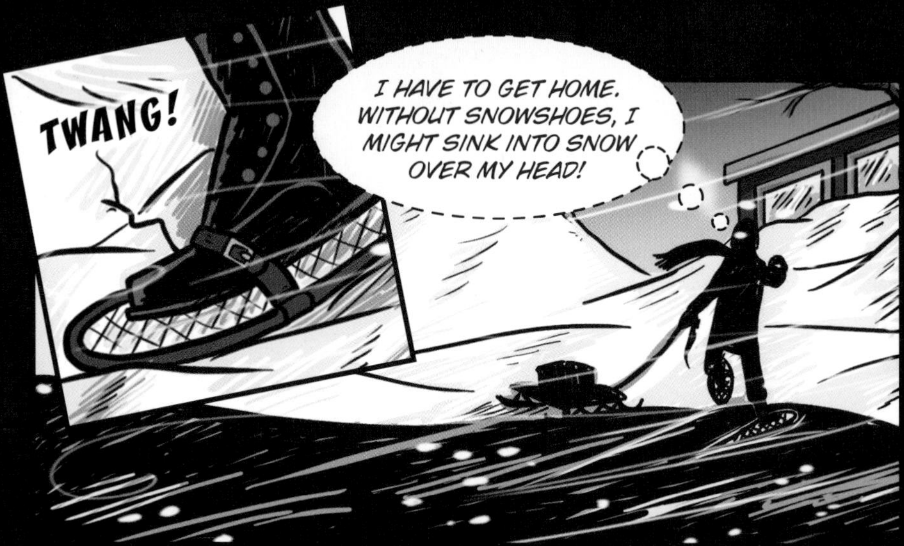
TWANG!
I HAVE TO GET HOME. WITHOUT SNOWSHOES, I MIGHT SINK INTO SNOW OVER MY HEAD!

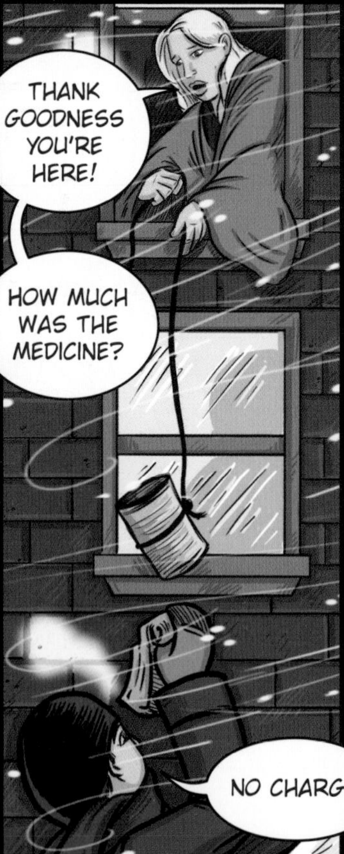
THANK GOODNESS YOU'RE HERE!
HOW MUCH WAS THE MEDICINE?
NO CHARGE.

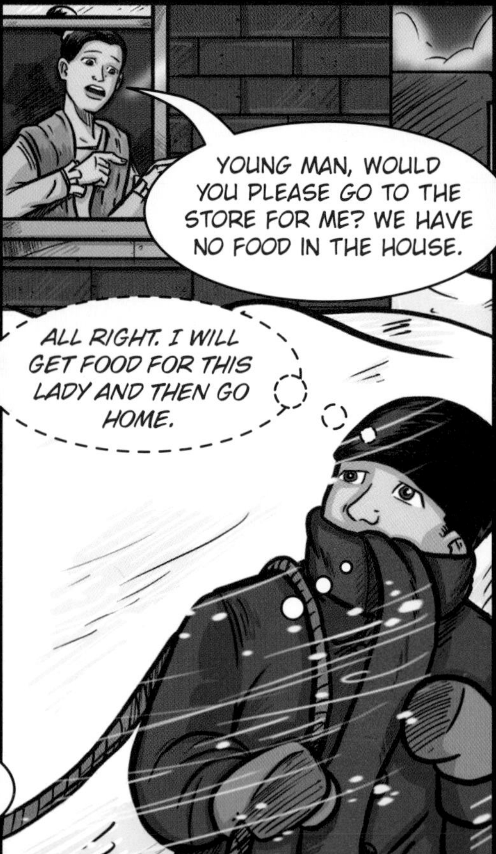
YOUNG MAN, WOULD YOU PLEASE GO TO THE STORE FOR ME? WE HAVE NO FOOD IN THE HOUSE.
ALL RIGHT. I WILL GET FOOD FOR THIS LADY AND THEN GO HOME.

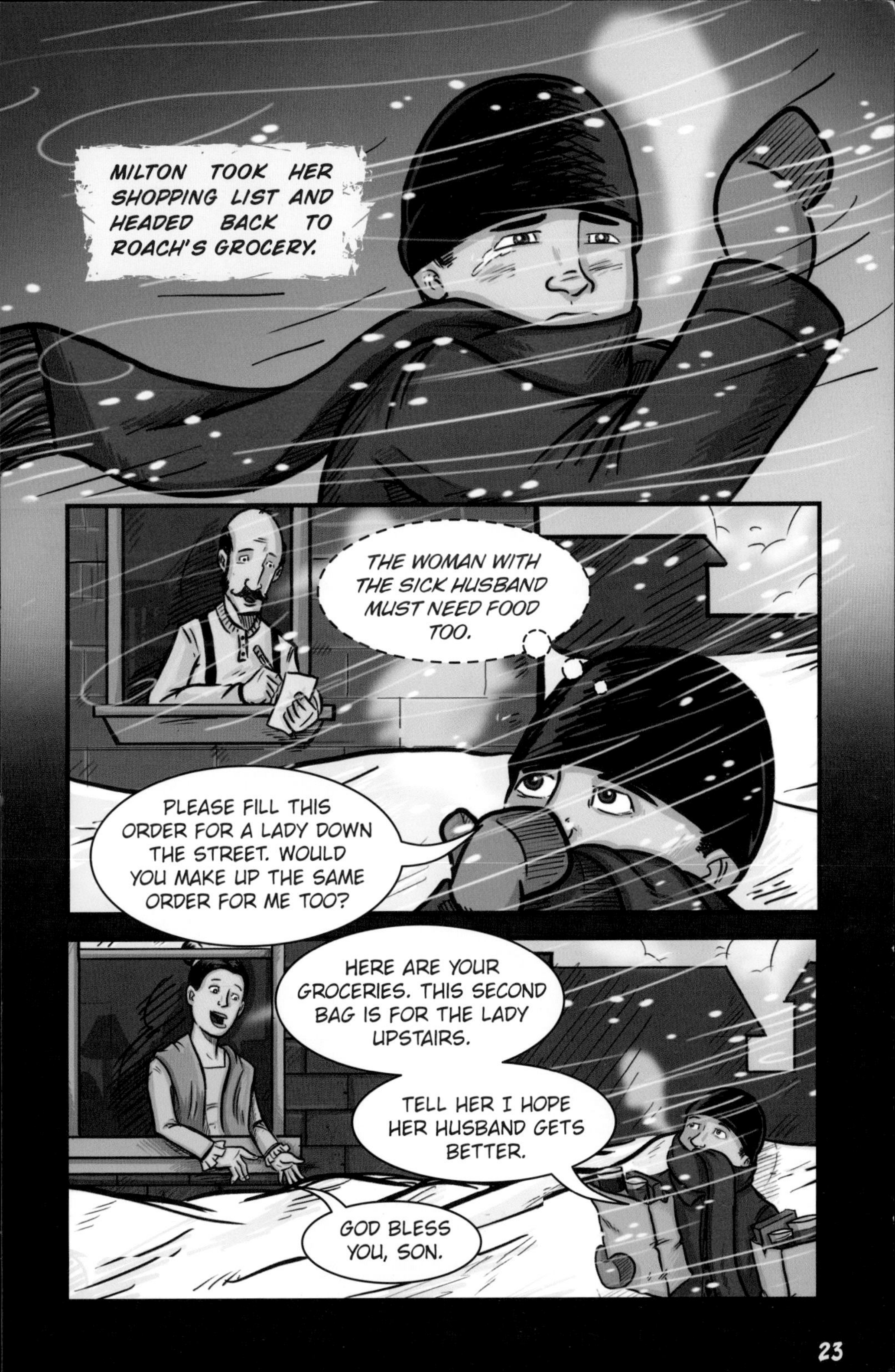
MILTON TOOK HER SHOPPING LIST AND HEADED BACK TO ROACH'S GROCERY.
THE WOMAN WITH THE SICK HUSBAND MUST NEED FOOD TOO.
PLEASE FILL THIS ORDER FOR A LADY DOWN THE STREET. WOULD YOU MAKE UP THE SAME ORDER FOR ME TOO?
HERE ARE YOUR GROCERIES. THIS SECOND BAG IS FOR THE LADY UPSTAIRS.
TELL HER I HOPE HER HUSBAND GETS BETTER.
GOD BLESS YOU, SON.

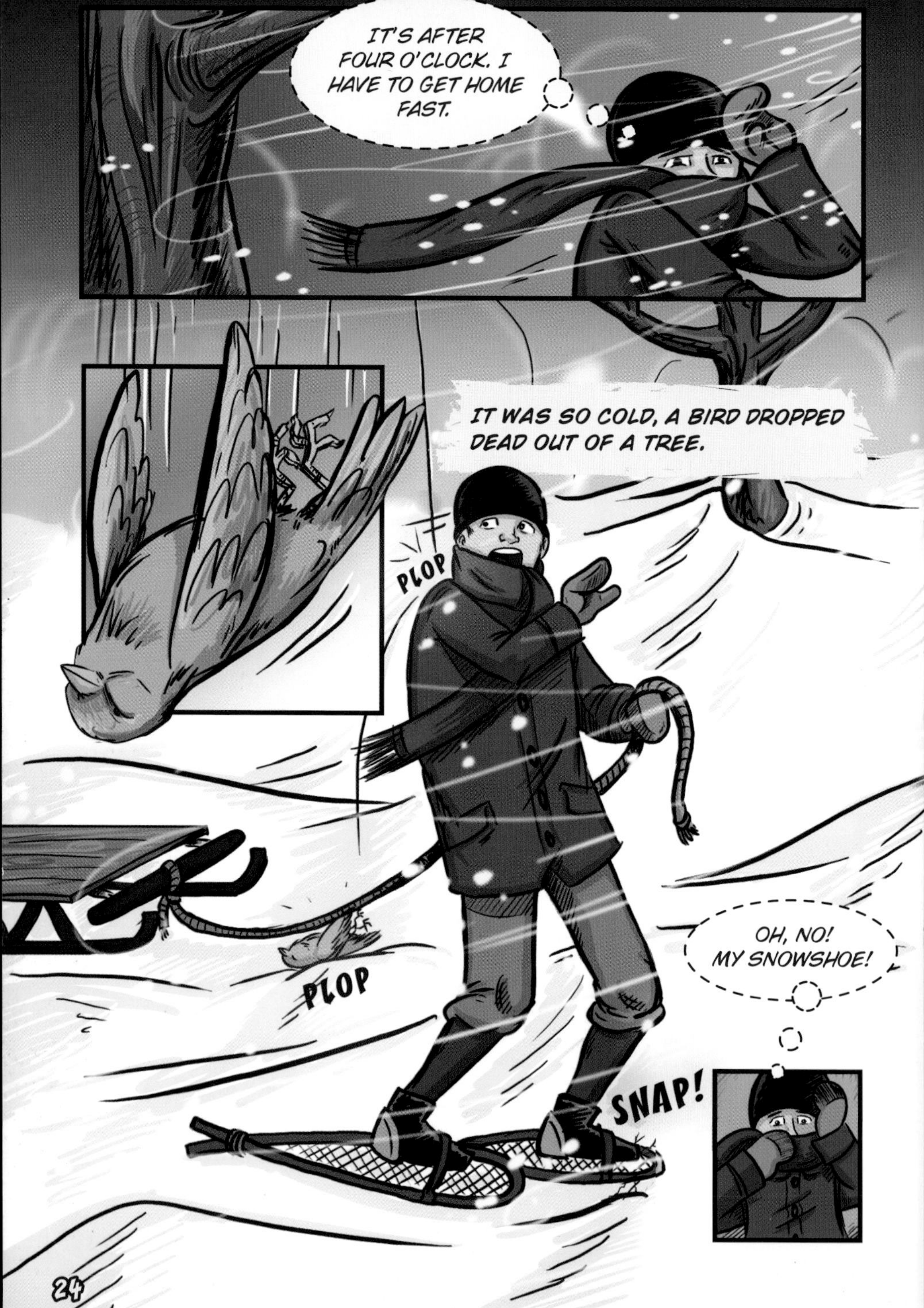
IT'S AFTER FOUR O'CLOCK. I HAVE TO GET HOME FAST.
IT WAS SO COLD, A BIRD DROPPED DEAD OUT OF A TREE.
PLOP
PLOP
OH, NO! MY SNOWSHOE!
SNAP!

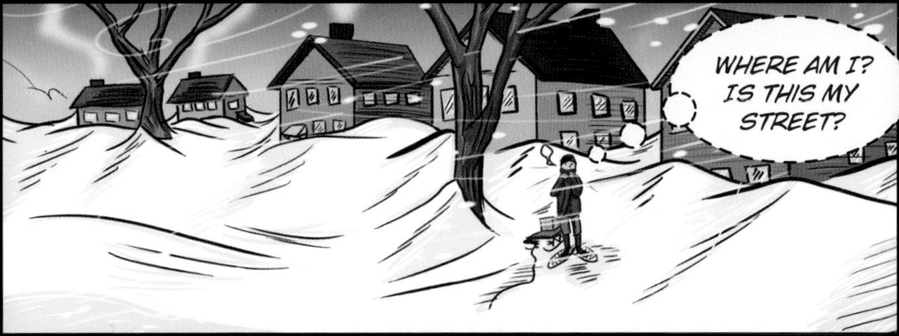
WHERE AM I? IS THIS MY STREET?

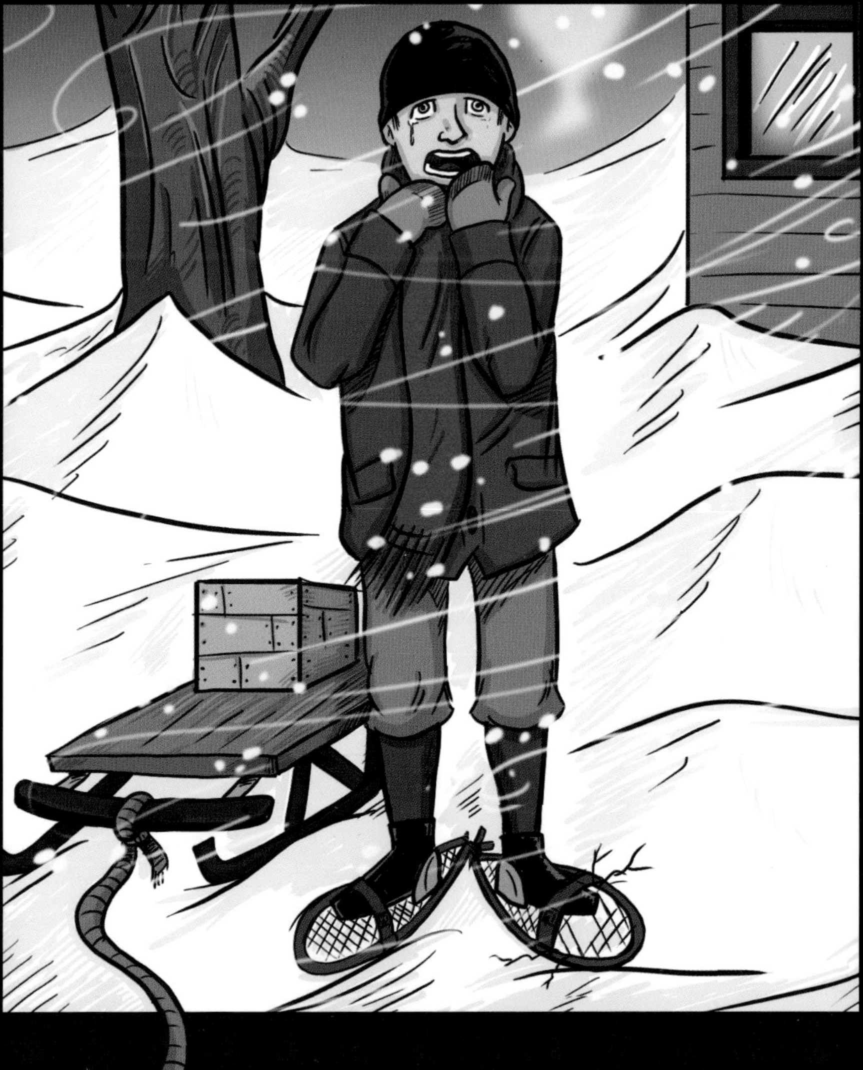

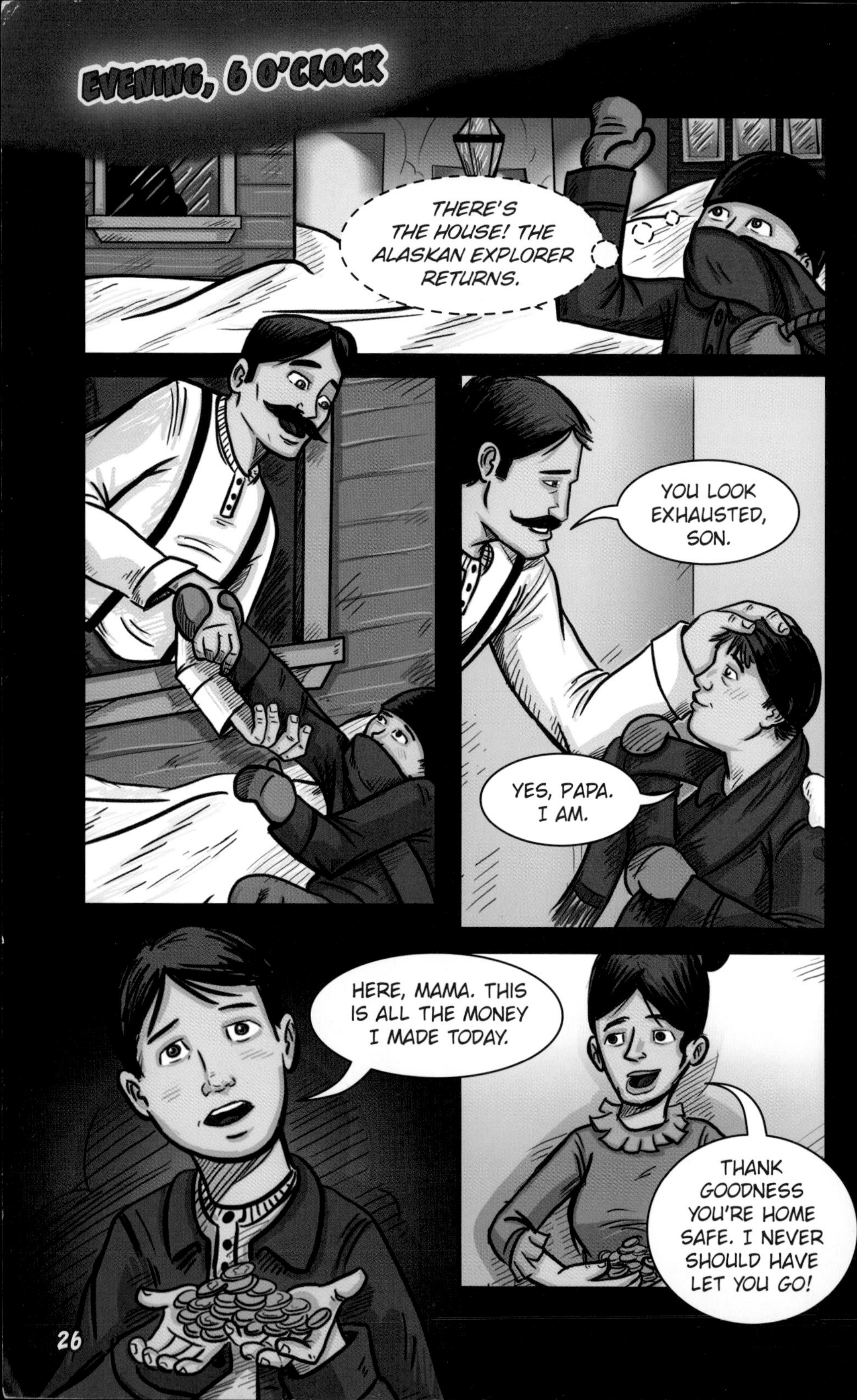
EVENING, 6 O'CLOCK
THERE'S THE HOUSE! THE ALASKAN EXPLORER RETURNS.
YOU LOOK EXHAUSTED, SON.
YES, PAPA. I AM.
HERE, MAMA. THIS IS ALL THE MONEY I MADE TODAY.
THANK GOODNESS YOU'RE HOME SAFE. I NEVER SHOULD HAVE LET YOU GO!

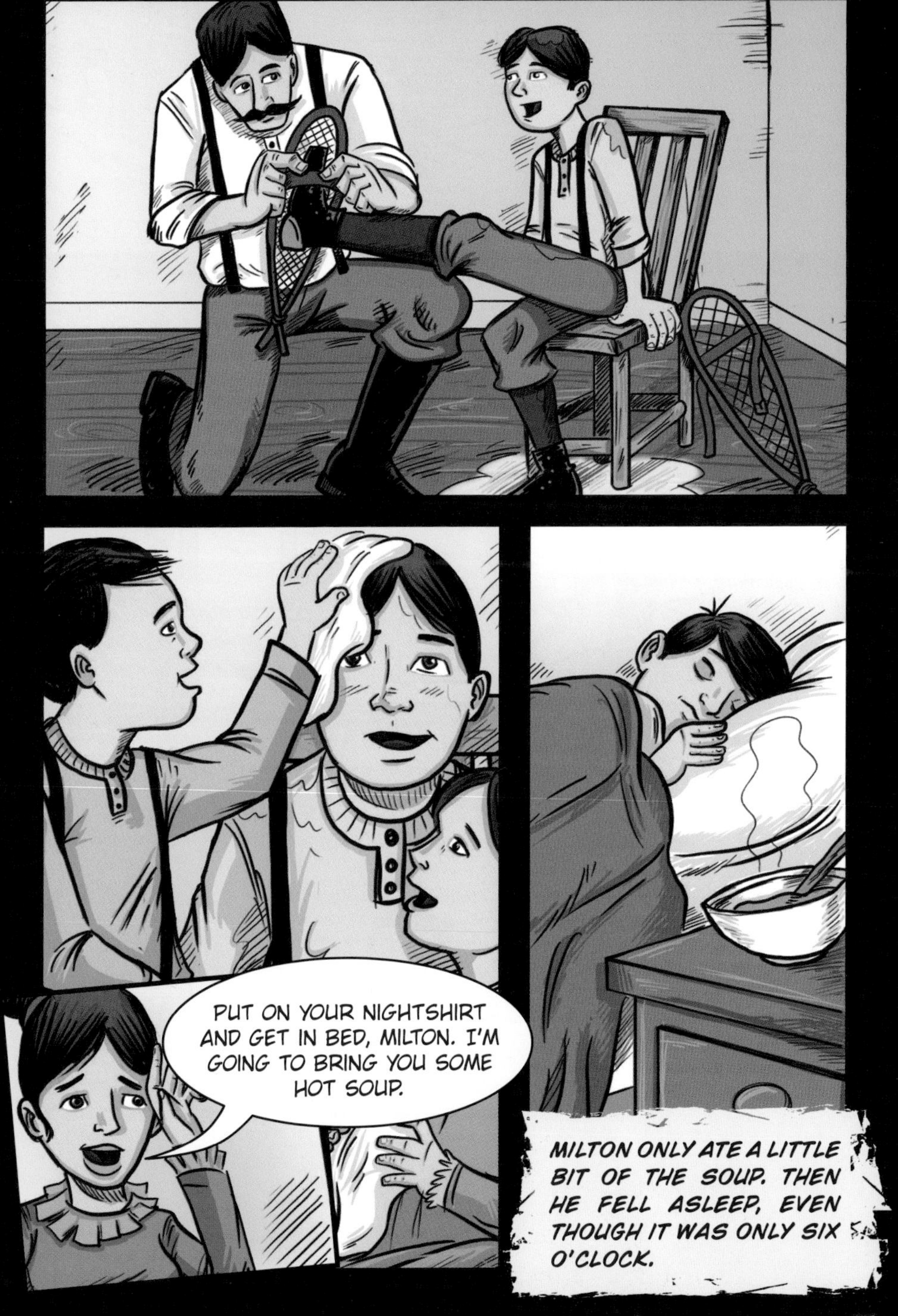
PUT ON YOUR NIGHTSHIRT AND GET IN BED, MILTON. I'M GOING TO BRING YOU SOME HOT SOUP.
MILTON ONLY ATE A LITTLE BIT OF THE SOUP. THEN HE FELL ASLEEP, EVEN THOUGH IT WAS ONLY SIX O'CLOCK.

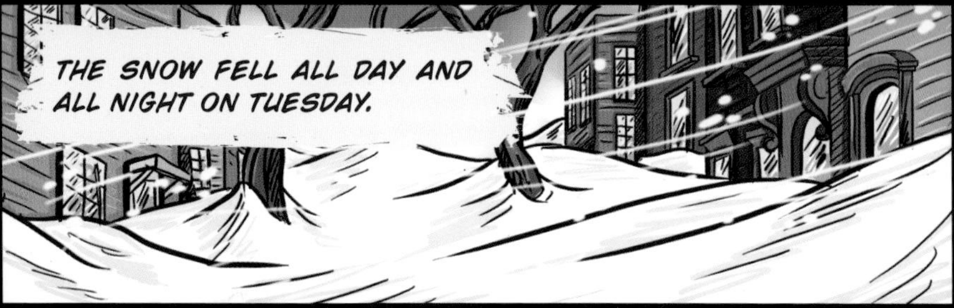
THE SNOW FELL ALL DAY AND ALL NIGHT ON TUESDAY.

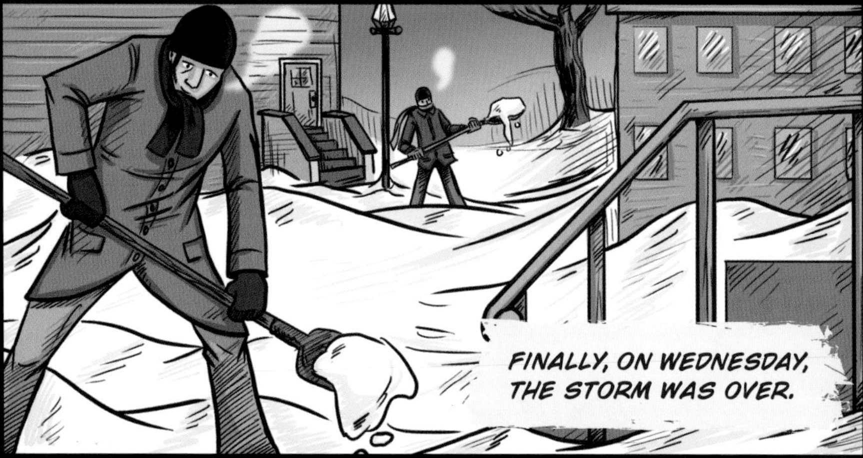
FINALLY, ON WEDNESDAY, THE STORM WAS OVER.

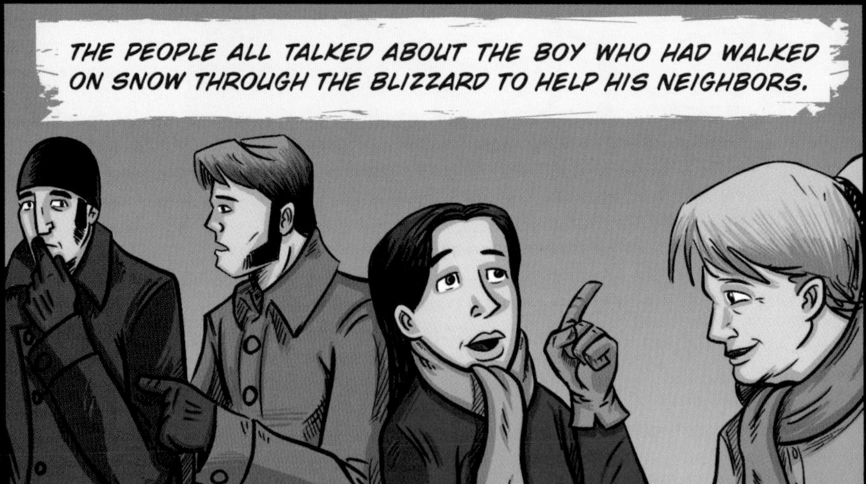
THE PEOPLE ALL TALKED ABOUT THE BOY WHO HAD WALKED ON SNOW THROUGH THE BLIZZARD TO HELP HIS NEIGHBORS.

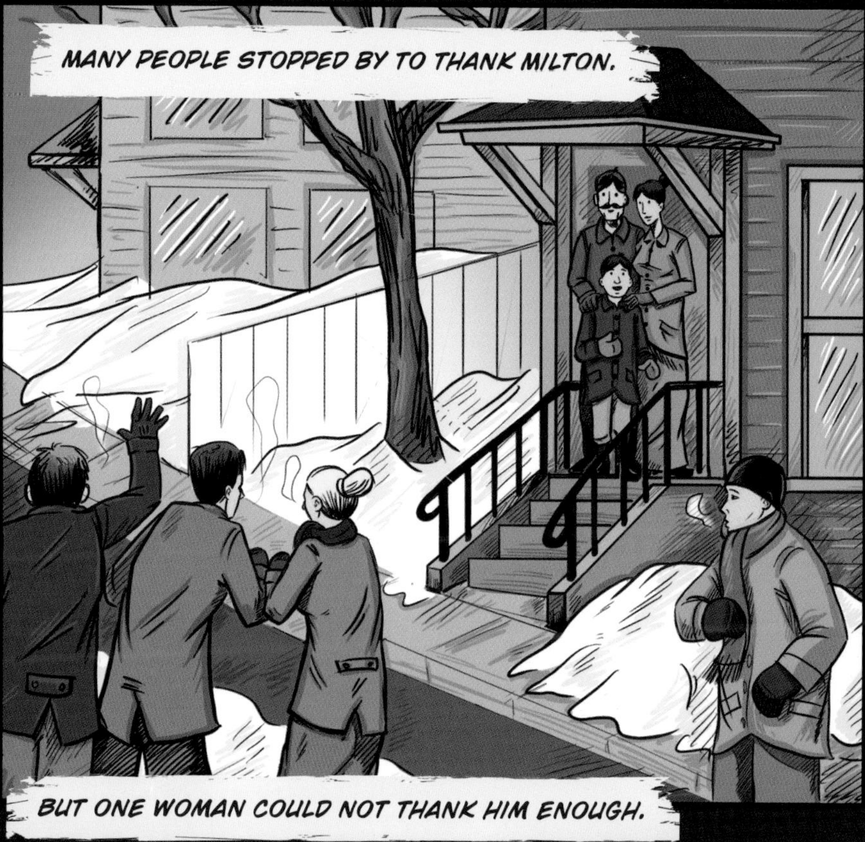
MANY PEOPLE STOPPED BY TO THANK MILTON.
BUT ONE WOMAN COULD NOT THANK HIM ENOUGH.

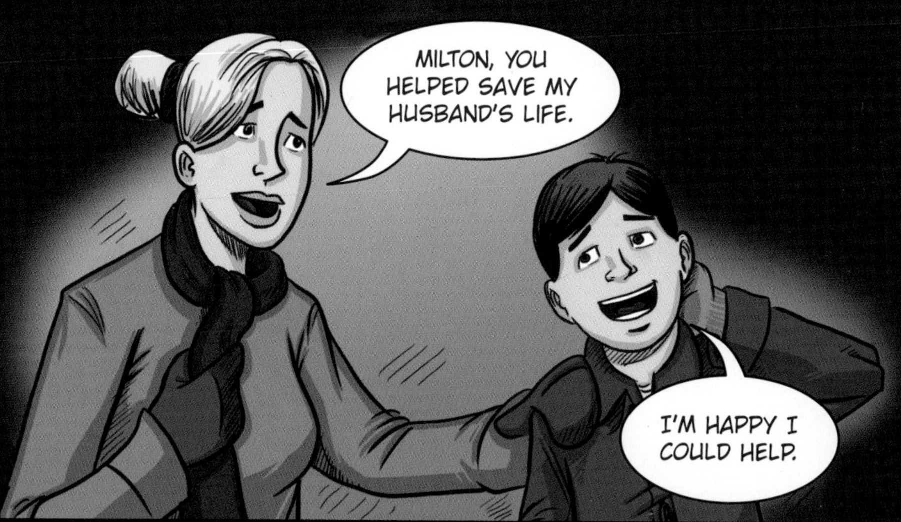
MILTON, YOU HELPED SAVE MY HUSBAND'S LIFE.
I'M HAPPY I COULD HELP.

AFTERWORD

THE 1888 BLIZZARD SET RECORDS THAT HAVE NOT BEEN BROKEN EVEN AFTER MORE THAN A HUNDRED YEARS. THE NORTHEASTERN UNITED STATES HAS NEVER AGAIN SEEN SUCH A HUGE SNOWFALL OVER SUCH A LARGE AREA. WIND SPEED, SNOW LEVELS, AND LOW TEMPERATURE RECORDS FOR DOZENS OF PLACES IN THE AREA STILL STAND. BESIDES THE MANY PEOPLE WHO SUFFERED FROM FROSTBITE, EXHAUSTION, AND INJURIES FROM FALLS, MORE THAN 400 PEOPLE DIED DURING THE STORM. NEVER BEFORE OR SINCE HAS A BLIZZARD IN THE UNITED STATES TAKEN SO MANY LIVES. STORIES OF THE STORM BECAME PART OF AMERICAN FOLKLORE.

MILTON DAUB, HIS FAMILY, AND HIS NEIGHBORS NEVER FORGOT HIS SNOW WALKING DURING THE GREAT BLIZZARD OF '88.